BURNING MAN

Chris DiCroce

Tin Finch

tinfinchpress.com

ISBN: 0692898174
ISBN-13: 978-0692898178

Join the Insider's List

Join the Chris DiCroce Insider's List for exclusive content and to be the first to find out about new releases, contests, and more. Visit chrisdicroce.com to join.

Burning Man Soundtrack

Get the official soundtrack to Burning Man, a handpicked selection of original songs from the author's three critically-acclaimed albums, for free. (Look for details at the end of the book.)

What They're Saying

"Chris DiCroce writes books the same way he composes and sings, from the soul."

"As talented a songwriter as Chris DiCroce is, it's no surprise that his foray into longer form prose is so well written."

Acknowledgments

Living and traveling on a 35-foot sailboat is a challenging endeavor on its own. Trying to complete any body of work while doing so is much like standing on a basketball. This book would not have seen the light of day without the assistance and artistry of a few dear friends.

To my wife, Melody DiCroce, thank you. You jumped off the bridge with me. Heart and soul. Editor, graphic designer, sounding board and cheerleader. You inspire and encourage me every single day. Dance with grace along the fine line between loving partner and professional corrector. Living with me in a space smaller than most people's bathroom deserves some sort of military commendation.

Special thanks to my friend Andrew Arnold for the astonishing cover image, *Hominis Incendium*. The amount of love and energy you infuse into your art is beyond compare. I am forever grateful and honored that you allow me to associate my work with yours.

A word of thanks to the Nelson Poynter Memorial Library at the University of South Florida Saint Petersburg. This wonderful library afforded me a space to work. It was quiet and close to the campus coffee shop. That is inspirational in and of itself. I do love my coffee.

Tom-Erik-Bockman-Pedersen, the "Real Dash." Thanks, my friend. I've pirated your nickname. Hopefully you'll be inundated with kooky fans. Welcome to the circus.

To friends, family, and the city of Nashville. Thanks for being part of my story.

Part One

one

Maybe it was the scotch; maybe it was his fifty-three years. Either way, Dash couldn't piss.

Could've been he didn't need to. Maybe he was just hiding; under the indictment of a single overhead halogen, waiting for the album to finish playing. After all, the two-inch thick, double-insulated door kept all the opinions on the other side.

His head was spinning from thirty years of feedback and now he had to walk out into the studio and pretend he could give a shit about what the music critics, managers, and socialites had to say. He already knew they wouldn't like it. Some were only there to see and be seen. Some to watch the fall. People love free booze and a car crash.

He flushed, grabbed his tumbler from the back of the toilet and leaned heavily on the handle. *Here we go*, he thought. The studio lounge was empty, except for a banquet table. Eviscerated smoked salmon platters and dirty napkin origami dotted the long table. Nestled among abandoned, watered-down, half-empty drinks were shrimp tails and the remains of partially eaten chocolate-covered strawberries.

Every good studio has a kitchen, but Emerald had a bar, and behind that bar stood the hired gun for the night. She was cute, her dark hair pulled back, slick in a ponytail. Her taut, well-packed blouse hinted from beneath the requisite black vest. She didn't notice Dash come out of the bathroom. Her busy thumbs abruptly halted when he gently cleared his throat.

"Oh my god," she said, "I'm sorry, Mr. Nelson. I didn't see you."

Dash smiled, "No problem. Sounds like the record's finished in there, ay?"

"Yes, seems like everyone loved it," she said, reaching for a clean tumbler. "Another?"

"Please. Double. My resolve for nights like these is bolstered by heavy pours."

She scooped up a handful of perfectly chipped ice. On the second shelf, below the microwave, Dash and Westie kept a bottle of Aberlour 12-year. Sweet, golden, with a hint of vanilla and a soft finish. The secret stash. The small iceberg didn't stand a chance.

"Right to the rim there please," Dash directed her with his finger.

"How's that?"

"Perfect," he said, pulling a crisp twenty from his shirt pocket.

"That's just..." he drew a sip to keep the liquid from spilling over the rim. "...perfect. Wish me luck."

He turned to head into the great room, stopping short to peer through the large glass door at the throngs of people drinking, laughing, talking. He couldn't hear a thing except the AC unit's dull hum in the lounge. The isolation doors were a thing to behold.

All those folks. All that noise. Nary a decibel making its way into the sanctuary of the lounge. At least not until TC opened the door and shattered the moment.

"Hey Dash, this record is amazing man!" He slurred through a mouthful of marbles, sweet northern California sinsemilla wafting from his person. TC Williams was the head of Artist Relations at Bottom Third Records and directly attached to Dash's catalog of music. With his cop mustache and long out-of-date rat tail, he looked more porn star than music exec.

"Hey TC, thank you. I appreciate you being here," Dash muttered through his teeth.

"Are you kidding? I wouldn't miss this night. Westie is really excited. We've been conspiring. We're here for you, Dash. We wanna make this record your biggest ever."

"Thank you, TC. Really. I'm excited too. I love the record and I'll...I'll let you and Westie hash out the plan." TC was currently blocking the door leading to the pass-through to the great room. The small isolation booth was a sonic black hole. Every word seemed to be vacuumed up into the booth's walls before they ever left one's mouth.

TC quipped, "Okay man, I gotta piss. I'll see you in a minute."

Dash stepped into the great room. Westie roared, raising a glass of scotch in his right hand and an unlit cigar in his left, "Here he is!" The entire room turned and erupted in hoots and applause. Dash stood smiling directly at Westie.

The great room at Emerald was forty feet wide and sixty feet long, with a ceiling high enough to shoot baskets. It was one of the few rooms big enough to track a small orchestra. A shimmering ebony Yamaha grand piano huddled, as best it could, in the corner, adorned with a hand-carved sign, "NO DRINKS."

The spirits of Johnny and Waylon stood watch over the Chi. The lyrics to Nashville Skyline clung perilously to the hundreds of breaths drawn in that historic room, elegantly decorated with lightly stained white oak floors and trim. The walls' whispers hushed under grey fabrics. The northeast corner of the room was finished out with stacked stone, its ledges and clefts sonically tuned for just the right amount of reflections. Sconces on dimmers set the right mood for the evening.

On this night, the white oak was blanketed by the

Persian rugs that Dash used on stage. Westie had the studio assistant stop by the band storage unit, unpack the tour rugs and bring them over. It was consummate West. Emerald, the place where Clutch was birthed was now the safe house for the unveiling of Dash's newest and best record yet.

The record had just finished playing. Westie made his way through the crowd to Dash. "Where ya been?" He said as he embraced Dash.

"I had to take a piss."

"For an hour?" Westie said, laughing.

"I'm an old man. Takes that long."

Dash waved as a few infidels began to softly shout, "Speech!" Westie was standing next to Dash, hand on his shoulder, grinning ear to ear. Dash hated moments like these. Westie loved every second.

Paul West wasn't just a manager. After thirty years, Westie was the keeper. The keeper of Dash's secrets and dreams. Fears and wishes. No father figure casting damp eyes to his boy's valedictory address felt a stronger sense of expanding pride than Westie did at that moment.

"Okay, old man," Westie said, patting him on the shoulder. "Flip the switch, Dash-man. Showtime."

Dash gulped at his scotch and wiped his mouth. He desperately wanted a cigarette but there was no smoking in the studio. As he set his glass down on a small wooden stool, the well-lubed crowd began clapping and shouting.

"Thanks..." Dash began. The room settled quickly. They knew Dash never shouted. They'd only get so much, for so long. "I...I wanna thank you guys for coming tonight. This means a lot." The room of about one hundred people erupted in cat calls and a smattering of applause.

"Westie," Dash looked at Westie who was immediately beside him. "Nice touch on the rugs." Westie raised his near-empty glass and bowed. "You're paying to have 'em cleaned." The room laughed. Westie rolled his eyes and chomped his unlit stogie.

"Now...I've been doing this—*we've* been doing this a long time. I've known a lot of you for almost thirty years and for that, I'm grateful. I'm grateful for the support you've given me and Westie. And, I'm grateful for the second chances. Third chances. Hell, I'm into double digits with some-a-you." The room was silent.

"I make records. I used to make hit records..." He glanced at Westie, "...but things change. Now, I just make—records. This record, Heavy Clutch, is as close to my heart as any of 'em. It's with some reservation that I came here tonight. I know you guys want...*Nashville* wants hit records. Well, I'm sorry. This one is gonna be a tough sell. Some of you gotta work this record. I didn't make it easy on ya. Some of you are gonna write your reviews tomorrow and...I want you to know...it's cool. I won't be offended if you rip me a new one."

Westie cleared his throat delicately. Dash took notice. "Sorry, West—I know you're having heart failure right now wondering what the hell I'm gonna say, but it's okay, friend." The room chuckled at the moment. Dash continued.

"I'm glad you're all here. I hope you enjoyed the food, the champagne, the scotch. I know I have. It's been a great run. This is the best record I've ever made. Now it's out there in the universe."

Dash grabbed his glass from the stool, and raised it in the air. He grabbed Westie in a firm, affectionate choke-hold and said, "I am certain of nothing but the holiness of the heart's affections and the truth of imagination. Thanks for coming, everybody."

Against the din of applause, Westie gave Dash a hug, "Keats?" He chuckled, "You end with Keats?"

"Yep. Keats."

"Well, holy shit, son. You've confused the hell out 'em twice tonight. Let's go smoke."

two

The two made their way through the lounge, Westie stopping to top off his scotch, draining the last of it. A load-in hallway led to two metal doors and the back parking area. Outside, a large eight-foot wall kept the curious star seekers out. It also kept out the breeze.

Dash pulled an American Spirit from his shirt pocket and offered one to Westie, who had chewed his stogie to death.

"Sure. I'll take one of those."

"West, I gotta tell ya man," Dash pulled from his cigarette, rattled his ice. "Radio's not gonna play this record. Letterman's gone. Leno's gone. Maybe you should get off while you can."

"Dash, we're gonna be fine. Fallon is the new Leno. He's a big fan. I've got calls in. The record drops next Tuesday. We're gonna be fine. Neither one of us has a rat-tail." The remark caught Dash off guard, and he laughed so hard he dropped his glass.

"Ah, shit—that's the last of it." Westie lightened the moment just as he'd wanted. "C'mon Dash. Let's go say goodnight to everyone. The food's gone. The scotch is gone. Party's over. Nobody hangs round when booze is gone."

As the metal doors slammed behind them, a figure stood at the end of the long hall. Dash knew that figure immediately. He missed that figure.

"Hello, Mrs. Nelson," Westie said as he embraced her in a long warm hug.

"Hi West," Jules said.

"I'll leave you guys alone. Dash? Jules?" Westie gestured to his glass. Jules declined.

"Yes. Whatever's left," Dash said, turning his attention back to his ex-wife.

"Hey babe. Thanks for coming. You look beautiful."

"Thanks," she said. The record is amazing. Really great, Dash. Songs are all you."

"Thank you. How you doing? I'm sorry I've been outta touch. It's been crazy."

"I know. It's been crazy for twenty years," she said with a smile.

"Yeah, it has. You been here for every minute of it. And I...I wanna say something, Jules." Dash's head was foggy. A night of memories rushed at him. The scotch, the adrenaline. The comedown. All now getting the better of him.

Jules put a gentle hand to his chest. "Not tonight. It's been a lovely evening. You haven't pissed anyone off. Why start now." Dash nodded. She leaned up into his frame and kissed his cheek, away from cameras, away from anyone who might speculate it was more than it was.

"I'm gonna go. It's late." She wiped the lipstick smudge. "Be careful, will you? I worry sick about you guys."

Westie arrived with two Heinekens dripping with condensation. "All that's left, my friend."

Jules tapped Westie on the chest, "Promise me you guys will call a car to take you home?"

"Will do, Jules." She gave Westie a sweet hug as he stood with the two beers. "Bye, Jules. It was great to see you." She smiled and disappeared down the long hallway, the swish of her strides carrying her scent out the twin metal doors.

"You guys need to..." Westie stopped himself.

"I know, West" Dash said, still focused on the doors. "What makes you so sure she'd have me back, anyway?"

"Man—I am many things. Blind ain't one of 'em. She looks at you the way she did when you got married. I'd venture to say a blind man could indeed see it. You, my good man, seem to be the only one who can't."

"Can we get outta here now?"

"Ah, yes. The change of subject cue. Yeah," Westie said. "I'll call the Major to come get us."

"I'm gonna drive."

"Dash, I just promised your ex-wife that we wouldn't drive."

"I'm good, Westie. I need the air. I'll be careful."

"Goddamn it," Westie said, "Take the car."

"You take the car, West. I'll see you in the morning." Dash said, already carrying a full head of steam through the lounge. Most of the crowd had dispersed. Westie, yammering into his cell, closed ranks and tried once more. "Dash, the Major is a few minutes away. He can drop you off first, then take me home. C'mon."

"Westie...I'm good." Dash grabbed him in a bear hug. "I love you, old friend. Thank you. For everything." He broke the embrace and kissed Westie on the face.

"Ah man, you're not good. You're drunk! Take...the damn...car."

Dash's face carried a short grin, completely enjoying the saunter across the parking lot to his 1986 Mercedes 560 SL. Within seconds the top was down and the radio up—loud. "Gotta love some Van the man!" Dash said over the music. Westie stood in the glow of the reverse lights and watched his friend back out.

"Let's have breakfast tomorrow." Dash said.

"I can't. I have a seven o'clock tee-time with Charlie." Dash waved. "Okay. Call me later."

With that, the black-on-black coupe made swift

through the large open gates, spreading a heavy glaze of Tupelo Honey the entire length of 17th Avenue.

three

From dead man to house-on-fire awake. Justice and Judge, two massive German Shepherds, shook the early morning calm with their booming barks as they lunged from the bed, feet pounding the hardwood floors, nails clawing as they skidded around turns and bounded down the stairs.

Dash's heart rate at coronary levels. Thick head, his blurry eyes made no connection with the motions his physical body was perpetrating. Echoing barks drowned out the knocking on the door. Dash tried desperately to focus his view of the Oceanaut upon his wrist but it wasn't yielding any secrets. Squinting towards the clock by the bed, 9:30am, he was still unsure if this was a dream—a cruel, cruel dream.

In last night's jeans and twisted, unbuttoned shirt, he managed to sit up, chasing back the urge to puke, wishing desperately those dogs would stop barking. "Judge! Justice! Goddamn it dogs. Shut...up!"

What the hell is going on, he thought. Justice and Judge whimpered and barked, clawing at the door. Then he heard it—the hard rapping on the door. At the same time, he heard the echo within the tall ceilings of his cell phone ringing. "Jesus Christ, this house better be burning down!" he shouted to the dogs as he staggered barefoot down the stairs. "I'm gonna make rugs outta you!"

When he jerked open the door, his confusion took him immediately back to bed, a dream. *I gotta be dreaming.*

"Jules?" Dash said, squinting into the morning sun, trying again to focus his vision. Justice and Judge squealed, knocking into Dash and Jules like cattle blasting through a gate too small.

"What's going on..." His eyes focused mid-sentence. Jules was crying. All the waters in all the oceans fell from her sweet, warm eyes.

"I'm sorry. I tried to call. We all tried to call. We've been texting you all morning." She began sobbing so hard her words were smothered. She wrapped herself tightly, in her own embrace, as if she were wearing a straight jacket.

"Jules...what the hell happened. Are you okay?" Dash had her by the shoulders staring into her red, swollen eyes.

"I was going to let myself in, but I...I..." Jules was staring the million-mile stare into the center of Dash's chest. His hangover was charging hard; a Brahma spewing snot and closing fast.

The dogs disappeared into the yard for their morning rounds.

"Jules, you're scaring me, love. Tell me what's going on. Are you hurt?"

She collected every molecule of self-control she could pluck from the chaos, and looked straight into Dash's foggy eyes. "Dash, Westie's dead."

He didn't hear that right. *Westie's dead? Nah, that can't be what she said.*

He looked at her face, searching for a hint that this was a really bad joke played on a hungover Dash. She wasn't giving him what he was searching for.

"Wha..." As if he'd been gut punched; the air wouldn't come, wouldn't form the words. "What...Jules..." Dash was searching the grounds, blinking desperately to rearrange the words that careened into a polymer skull. He turned from Jules, into the foyer, grabbed the banister.

Jules followed him inside. "He was supposed to meet Charlie at seven. They had a tee time. He didn't show up. You know West never misses a tee time. He's never late." Dash sat on the bottom step, trying to coax moisture into his mouth.

"Charlie texted him, called him, and—got no answer.

He got worried. He went to the house." Jules started crying again, "Charlie was the one who...he...Westie was on the floor." Jules knelt in front of Dash, her hands on his knees, her forehead to his, "I'm sorry baby. I'm so sorry."

"Where is he now?" Dash asked, wiping his eyes.

"He's at Vanderbilt. Charlie and Gary are there. They tried to resuscitate but...they pronounced him..." She didn't finish.

"Okay...I'll, uh, I'll get dressed and get over there." They walked to the door. "I'll meet you back at the hospital." Dash stopped and touched her shoulder. "Jules, don't let 'em take West anywhere. Let me get the dogs in...I'm right behind you."

* * *

Vanderbilt Medical Center sits in the middle of Nashville. The streets are crowded and the satellite parking lots are too far away to be convenient in an emergency. Dash swung the 560 into a spot just outside the emergency doors. A spot reserved for Dr. Emma Watkins.

He didn't bother to put the top up and he didn't do a check in the rearview to see just how rough he looked. As he approached the automatic doors, the sun showed a reflection that confirmed everything he needed to know. He pulled down his Ray-Bans and readied himself for the barrage. The gawkers, whispering voices.

Jules met him at the information desk. He grabbed her hand and the two of them walked past the onlookers to the elevator. When the doors opened on the third floor, Charlie Tate, Dash's tour manager and Westie's golf partner, and Gary Smith were standing in the hallway. Charlie sipped coffee from a small Styrofoam cup while Gary spoke into his phone in a hushed voice.

Dash was slow. Imaginary viruses attacked his brain. The stench of infection stiffened his limbs. He hated hospitals. Jules gave him a gentle nudge out of the elevator. Charlie tried to smile. Gary hung up.

"Hey, Dash." Charlie hugged Dash and then Jules. Gary Smith was the elder of the group. The business manager, wise beyond his years, the voice of reason on many occasions. Methodical and measured. His eyes red, his smile, tight-lipped.

"I'm sorry Dash. I'm... very sorry."

"Gary...Charlie...We're all sorry. Westie was family. Our family." The group came together in an embrace.

"You want some coffee, Dash?"

"Yeah Charlie, that'd be great."

Dash walked over to the immense wooden door and gently rubbed the placard with a braille room number.

"Can I see him?"

"You can see him if you want." The voice was

unfamiliar. Dash turned to see a young doctor standing with his hands in his pockets. Gary did the introduction, "Dash, this is Dr. Romanowski. He's the one who tried to resuscitate."

"Mr. Nelson, I'm sorry for your loss. I am a fan. I know what Mr. West meant to you."

"Thanks. Call me Dash, please. I wanna see him for a minute."

"That's not a problem. We will need to move him down to the..." Romanowski stopped himself. "You take all the time you need, Dash." Dash glanced to Gary and Jules for reassurance, then pushed on the heavy wooden door.

Westie was lying completely flat in the sterile bed. No signs of activity. No defibrillators, no adrenaline needles. Nothing but Westie, tucked in neatly, the sheet to just below his bare shoulders. Eyes closed. It looked like he was smiling. Dash stood in the shadows of the room looking at his best friend's face, glowing in the soft white light.

It was cold. He noticed the hum of the AC unit. It's soft current of air trickled down his forehead and dried his eyes. It smelled like mouthwash. He realized he could still feel the sensation of those braille room numbers on his fingertips. He didn't want to look at Westie anymore.

Out in the hallway, the three were talking quietly when Dash came out of the room. "Here's your coffee."

Dash closed his eyes and sipped as if it was the first cup of coffee he'd ever tasted.

"Thank you, Charlie. Gary, does the press know? Has anyone released this to the media?"

Gary shook his head. "No," he said, "We were waiting 'til you got here."

"Good. I need a few hours."

Everyone looked confused. Charlie had been with Dash and Westie for almost twenty years. He was loyal, courteous and an all-around quiet southern boy. Never cussed, never made a fuss, and never questioned Dash. Until now. "Why not release it? The people are gonna wanna know."

"Charlie...Gary...I need some time." Dash looked Jules in the eye. She was unsure of what was happening.

"Dash," she said, "With Twitter and Facebook, this is gonna get out, if it hasn't already. People in this hospital... You know how it is."

"Listen, I'm just asking that nobody in our camp release this information. I gotta go by Westie's house. Dash took long, measured strides toward the elevator. He turned just long enough to let the words escape. "It's gonna be a long day."

Dash hit the button, desperately seeking the ground floor and an exit from the hospital. When he breached the emergency room doors, he was greeted by a tow truck—and an irritated Dr. Watkins.

"This you?" A lamp post would fill out a pair of coveralls better than that driver.

"Yeah, I'm on my way out," Dash said.

"You know, these signs are here for a reason," Dr. Watkins chimed in. Dash didn't pay the comment any mind. Sliding slowly into the seat, he twisted hard on the key and without missing a beat, as the car drifted backwards out of the spot he shot, "I'm a singer. I don't read too good."

four

Dash punched in the gate code, 0-6-2-1, Westie's birthday, and drove up the aggregate driveway. The two-story timber-frame, shaded by hackberries and tall oaks, rested atop a small rise on ten acres in west Nashville. A good wad of spit on a windless day could reach the well-stocked pond from the driveway. In winter, when the trees lost leaves, you could see the Batman building from the front porch.

It was from that very porch Dash stood, taking in all that was around him, celluloid clicking through the gate in his mind. What was gonna come now? Westie was dead. And that was just the beginning.

How am I ever gonna explain this, Dash thought as he opened the front door.

Any settling of the house happened years before. The floorboards were firm under foot, silent, save for boot heels. As many times as he had been to the house, he rarely had the occasion to visit Westie's bedroom. It felt weird. The bed was unmade, life was still hanging around.

Dash grabbed some underwear, jeans, Westie's favorite sweatshirt, and a KEY WEST embossed baseball cap. On his way out of the room, his eye stopped on an old photo of Westie, Dash, and Jimmy Buffett on Buffett's boat. Westie and Jimmy could have been twins. Each of them was tan and smiling...happy.

In Westie's office, the monolithic desk was immediately noticeable as too big for the room. Covered as it was in stacks of pages, it resembled a wake of turkey vultures perched upon a dead calf.

Dry-erase calendars adorned the west wall. Yellow Post-It notes were stamped haphazardly around the room. Tour schedules and pending contracts stuck to a corkboard above his filing cabinet. A Scotty Cameron prototype putter rested by the door frame, ready for duty. Dash's boot tip sent a crisp white Titleist pin balling off the baseboard. The walls were adorned with life—Dash's life. A roadmap from youth to love handles.

Dash began talking to himself, "Jesus, West, who's gonna go through all this shit?"

Dash flicked a dusty Rolodex overflowing with business cards. Westie's almost-empty coffee mug with a small halo of curdled cream drawing an outline of the state of Michigan. The ashtray, overflowing with thick cigar ashes; Westie's chewed stogie, and a roach that Dash picked up and lit.

"Oh West...you old son-of-a-bitch. You got out first. What am I gonna do without 'cha? How the hell am I gonna pull this off?" Dash walked to the window, gently yanked the string that opened the slatted ailerons, letting in shafts of light to illuminate the lingering smoke.

"Its gonna get interesting my friend. Very interesting." Dash knelt and moved a stack of papers, blocking the safe.

The Browning Titanium pressed a deep imprint into the carpet. Dash knew all about the S & G electronic lock because Westie went on and on about it. With each button, the keypad chirped its approval: R.E.G.G.I.E.

The stainless steel 5-spoke handle spun effortlessly, but the door didn't budge. Dash had to put his weight into getting the small door to open. He sat back, took a last draw from the suffocating joint, his fingers singed from the ember. He exhaled into the shafts of sunlight, licked his thumb and snubbed out the smoldering fleck.

Reaching into the safe, his head dense with weed and loss, he started to laugh. The tattered, brown paper-bag containing three hundred thousand dollars in meticulously banded stacks of cash had been rolled and crumpled, crammed, stashed and mashed into that safe for eons.

The cash itself was crisp. Brand new fragrant bills, bundled to perfection. The last bunch tumbled from the bag. Dash noticed, what else, a Post-It note. It read:

TAG, YOU'RE IT!
DON'T FORGET THE BOX!

Dash leaned forward again, into the safe. Numb fingers felt the sharp corners on the impressive little black cube. His smirk grew; tears filled his eyes when the lid revealed its contents. He began to cry and laugh at the same time.

Pulling the sparkling Rolex from the box, an umbilical cord of light blue thread was fastened to the band. He pulled, and from under the silk packing material came a small card, written in Westie's handwriting;

If you're holding this, I'm gone and you're not. A deal's a deal. Know this, my friend. You're a bright shining star in a cloudy world. Don't waste any more time. It's precious. I miss you, pal.

Love, Westie

Dash threw his old watch in the safe and put on the Rolex. Wiping tears away, he picked up Westie's landline and dialed Gary Smith's cell.

"Hey Gary, it's Dash. I know...sorry for calling from Westie's line. You at the office? I'm on my way. I'm gonna need you to set up an offshore account."

five

There was no shady math with Gary Smith or his company. Gary didn't need an immediate explanation from Dash. He didn't seek the whys or what-for. The only thing that good ol' Kentucky boy needed was assurance.

"We've worked together a long time, Dash. I know you and West have had your crazy moments. I know you two had your island hide-outs and Butch Cassidy adventures, but I'm at the end of my rider here. I don't need any surprises to bite me on the ass… we clear?"

Dash said, "Crystal."

Spending the better part of the day at Gary's office, Dash learned more about registered agents and international havens than he ever cared to know. He needed to get out of there. He needed a shower. Justice and Judge needed to eat. Their stomachs functioned with Swiss watch precision.

The 560 swung up to the front gates just after 5pm. Dash hit the automatic garage door opener as they closed behind him. The two massive canines stormed across the lawn and met the car halfway up the driveway. Judge had developed the bad habit of leaping into the moving car. An event that usually ended with some sort of automotive vandalism.

Dash always went in through the garage, which dumped him into the large, modern, under-decorated kitchen. Two years before, when the divorce was final, he bought the place from Brit rocker Tommy Crane. Among others, Tommy had ideological issues and found great difficulty in paying taxes. While tall fences and guns do wonders to keep adoring fans at bay, they do little in the virtual world of financial seizures.

Tommy was okay with relinquishing the asset. He sent word from the south of France that of all the possible "assholes on the planet" that could have taken possession, he was happy Dash stole it out from under all of them. Gary was the one responsible for pulling off the deal, and while the six-thousand square feet were five-thousand more than Dash needed, it was a deal not to be missed.

The pièce de ré·sis·tance was the eight-hundred-square-foot studio. Before the seizure, Tommy's road crew absconded with guitars, clothes, and anything else they could load into the road trucks. They cleared the place out in a dark-of-night heist, but left behind the Trident Series 80 console, a classic B3 purchased from Winwood after his Arc of a Diver record, mics, cables and stands. Sacrilege. A frivolous retreat.

A sea of wide plank walnut floors played out through the vacant museum, its surge interrupted momentarily by the single overstuffed couch the middle of the formal living room. The dogs claimed the hand-stitched leather island as sovereign domain.

Jules had ordered the couch. She ordered the bedroom set and the contemporary kitchen set, too. Because Dash would never do it. He hovered endlessly in the studio.

The seven other rooms were empty except for Dash's Persian rugs. Rugs stacked on top of rugs in each room. Silk, wool, some hand-dyed with organic vegetable coloring. Rugs from Iran, Bahrain, Pakistan, Iraq and Russia. Each time he traveled to Asia or the Far East, he shipped back the "expensive dog beds."

He dropped his keys on the counter by the fridge, grabbed a cold beer and tossed two huge scoops of organic salmon-and-sweet-potato kibble into the stainless bowls. One for Justice. One for Judge.

Dash stepped heavily. Purposefully. He undressed as he made his way up the stairs, two at a time. His Heineken foamed and left a trail to the shower. He tossed his jeans and boxers on the bed, spun the handle and doused his head in the steaming hot water. "This has been one hell of a day," he said to himself. Half of the green bottle's contents disappeared in one swig. He set the bottle on the soap dish out of danger from the spray.

Dash was beginning to feel the outer bands. The barometer was falling. He could feel it in his ears. He stood, arms extended, one palm on the north wall of the shower, one on the south, as if Dali had captured the exact moment when Dash succumbed to the torrent of warm water washing through the crack in his ass.

Thirty minutes later, cleanest he would be for days, he pulled on a fresh pair of boxers and well-crushed Levi's. Barefoot and shirtless, he swiped the condensation from the massive mirror. His tired face stared back. In a barely audible voice, he said, "You need a vacation, you old bastard."

He pulled a fresh razor across his face as if it were his wedding day. He rinsed the razor and tossed it into his dopp kit, along with some deodorant. He grabbed his favorite canvas backpack and threw in an extra pair of jeans, boxers and a crisp black t-shirt. From the top of his dresser, he grabbed a well-worn passport, pulled his wallet from the jeans on the bed and took a quick look around.

Justice and Judge followed Dash down the stairs as they always did. On the way through the kitchen, he grabbed another Heineken, pulled on his boots, his shirt, and patted the dogs farewell.

Sitting in the topless Benz, his wet hair dripping onto the screen of his iPhone, he typed Jules a text.

"Hi! Need a favor. Can you watch the dogs? Couple days."

It was almost 6. The late-day sun was low and still warm. Creamy, face-sized magnolia blossoms dripped their coital perfume—strong, like knockout drops, and a lavender sky gave no hints.

He finished off the second beer, spun the Benz around and slid the empty bottle underneath the passenger seat.

six

When Dash arrived back at Vanderbilt Medical Center, it was dark. Delaying his arrival further, he'd made a quick stop at Bobby's Idle Hour for a whiskey, which turned into three whiskeys. Which turned into three whiskeys and two more Heinekens. He had been circling for an hour, trying to find the right place to park. At least that's what he was telling himself.

And for all his intoxication, it took almost twenty minutes to get the top up. An exercise, when undertaken in any manner of sobriety, usually occupied about four.

His phone lit up with a response from Jules. "Sorry, just got this. Sure. Everything ok?"

Dash typed a haphazard, "Yeah. Thanks. Talk soon."

Leaning hard against the car, Dash lit a cigarette and said to himself, "I need another drink." There were few things in the universe he needed less. "What kinda crazy sons-a-bitches do such a thing?" He was drunk, talking out loud. He looked around to see if anyone noticed the crazy man arguing with a ghost. The crazy man with an uncanny resemblance to Dash Nelson, the famous singer.

There is nothing so evident as a drunk trying to walk like he's sober. Upright, stiff and prancing like a Tennessee walking horse, he approached the door, heart racing, breath shallow. Another of those outer bands had arrived.

The nondescript building was hard to find on Google Maps, but he believed his thumbs stumbled upon the right place. Once inside, he was certain. The tile might not have started out that particular shade of yellow, but it reminded him of his high school locker room. Neither a place nor time he cared to revisit. And if a collection of dead, decomposing bodies didn't make the space grim enough, the florescent lighting selection currently illuminating the passageway did.

He could feel his heartbeat. He could hear it. He'd swear it was drowning out the clicks his suede boots made when he shuffled his drunken feet. A marionette grateful for the puppeteer's precision.

A set of double doors met him halfway down the hall. Just as he pressed his forehead against the glass window of the right door, the left door swung into him, "Holy shit!" He sprung like a cat hit with sixty volts.

"Can I help you?" a young man said, calmly picking up the clipboard that Dash sent spinning from his grip.

"You scared the living hell outta me." Dash said.

"Well sir, living hell is an odd choice of words in a morgue."

"Yeah, I...I...guess. Listen, are you the guy in charge?"

"No, Dr. McFadden is," the young man mumbled. "But he went to Starbucks. He had a gift card. I'm Christian. Not the religion."

"Ah, okay, Christian." Dash tried to collect himself, "My friend Westie...Paul West is here. He died today and...I didn't get to see him earlier. I was wondering if I might be able to say...you know, goodbye."

Christian waved his free hand in front of his face, trying to disperse the alcohol breath, "Oh, sir, now is not a good time. Your friend has been in the cooler for several hours now. He's...how can I put this...very dead."

"Look, I know he's dead. It's very important that I see him. He's my best friend. He's been my business partner for thirty years. Have a heart, kid." Dash pulled a crisp hundred-dollar bill from his pocket. "Have a heart." Dash's celebrity was clearly invisible to the millennial, and that was just fine with him.

Christian eyed Dash incredulously. With little hesitation, he scanned the hallway, darted his eyes, grabbed the c-note from Dash's grasp. "You have fifteen minutes."

Christian led Dash to a large room with more of the same yellow tile and four stainless steel lab tables. On a table lay a large black zippered bag. Christian approached the bag, grabbed the zipper with zero delicacy, and with what some might consider violence, revealed Westie's dead body.

"Here he is. Sorry about the HRP."

Dash was a bit taken aback. "I'm sorry...HRP?"

"Human Remains Pouch," Christian said in an unaffected-by-death voice. Leaving Dash and Westie, Christian reached for the door, turning with one last thought, "I'm sorry you lost your friend."

Dash fixated on the door as he dressed West in the clothes he had gathered from his house. The body was already stiff and uncooperative.

"Goddamn man...this is fucking nuts." Dash whispered to himself as he struggled to move the limbs to get his boxers and jeans on.

"Westie, I always thought I'd be taking care of you when you got old, but not like this, man. Not like this." He managed to get Westie's body dressed. "Now how the hell do I get us outta here?" Looking at his watch, he had about four minutes before his fifteen minutes would be up.

The asylum-like room had two large windows on the

wall opposite the door, about seven feet off the ground. Dash leaned into the table with all his weight. He didn't expect it to roll so easily. Dash, the table, and Westie all met the depressing yellow tile at great speed. The crash was loud. The racket was sure to rouse Christian from his masturbatorial haze.

"Goddammit!" Dash was frantic. Jumping up onto the table, straddling his dead friend and manager, he unlocked the window and pushed with all his weight. The window blasted open. The pressure exerted on the window caused the table to drift from the wall, and Dash crashed to the linoleum with a resounding thud. He managed to mute any scream that wanted to burst from his lungs as he coaxed his inebriated frame back to his feet. He then realized how high the window was. Time was fleeting.

Wincing, stammering like Frazier in Manila, he pulled the table with Westie back to the window. Again straddling his old mate, with one huge thrust Dash got Westie's torso out the window. "I'm sorry, buddy," Dash gasped breathlessly. "This...is...gonna..." He shoved. And like an old Christmas spruce, the rest of Westie went tumbling from the window, landing on the hard ground with a crackling thump.

"...hurt."

Dash was drenched with sweat. His shirt's pearl snaps had come undone in the struggle. He tossed his canvas backpack through the window and hopped up into the frame, legs dangling. Stuck. His belt caught the latch. The jump forced the table to travel across the room into the other metal tables, leaving Dash hanging like the amateur trapeze artist he never dreamed of being.

"Holy mother of..." before he could finish the sentence, he felt a sudden release. He heard the belt pop and quickly realized he was head over heels, tumbling to the dirt.

Dash landed on Westie. Not wasting a single second, he spun himself up like an offensive lineman trying to win a starting job, hauled Westie's stiff, battered body up over his shoulder, and fireman-carried him across the campus toward his car. Short on breath and whispering to his dead friend, he said, "You know pal..." gasping for air, "they tend...to frown...on hauling dead bodies...across the campus." He started to laugh, "Goddamn it, West. I'm too old for this shit."

With Westie in the passenger seat, Dash gently plopped the faded Key West cap onto Westie's noggin. It was only then that he realized his friend was infinitely—

Permanently.

Gone.

Westie sat stiff with closed eyes. No smile anymore. Dash lit a cigarette, started the car and buckled in his best friend. "Safety first, partner. Safety first."

seven

When Charlie saw the headlights coming up the driveway, he knew instantly who it was. The night sky was black at Charlie's place. None of the city's afterglow reached his gate.

The son of a preacher, Charlie had the blood of the Cherokee beating through the heart of an Irishman. A quietness about him; a calm hand. Nobody could ever figure out why a guy like Charlie would want to work in the chaotic ballet of egos and drama queens. The long stints on the road, occupying the spaces between setting up the blocks and taking down the blocks, served as the grease that kept Charlie's wheels from squeaking. He was the ringleader. He managed the movement of the band and crew. He reminded everyone of just how lucky they were and he did it without ever saying a word. He kept plates spinning, wheels rolling and the doors on time.

In his crisp white t-shirt, baggy jeans, and bare feet, he gently pushed the screen door open to greet the old Benz as it skidded to a stop. The dust cloud overtook the headlights. White spotlights lingered on Charlie's retinas. He hung tight on the porch, a Budweiser, one of many for the night, in hand.

"Hey Charlie," Dash said, as he opened the door and wrestled his drunk frame upright.

"Hey Dash." Considering the day's events, Charlie wasn't surprised to see Dash at such an hour. "You want a beer?"

Dash nodded his head, "Yes...I want two beers."

Charlie chuckled. The screen door slammed behind him. From the fridge, he grabbed a Budweiser. He pulled two tumblers from the cabinet, poured three fingers of Blanton's in each and returned to the porch. Dash was standing at the bottom of the steps, still wearing his Ray-Bans; winded, one foot up on the second step, hands on his knee.

"You okay, Dash?" Charlie said, handing him the beer and whiskey.

"Oh yeah," Dash said, gulping the better part of the Blanton's. "Been a long day, Charlie. Long day."

Charlie pulled out a pack of Marlboro reds and offered the pack to Dash.

"Charlie, I need your truck," Dash said, through a long exhale of smoke, scattering the moths around the porch lights.

"You need my truck now?" Charlie said.

"Yeah...can I...can I borrow your truck, Charlie?"

"Well Dash, you...uh, you know you're welcome to my truck anytime, but...you seem a little outta sorts right now. You sure you need it right this second?"

"Yes, Charlie. Yes, I'm outta sorts. I'm drunker than Cooter Brown. And yes, I need it right this second." Dash tried his best to control his sway. "Look man, you have my word. You'll getchur truck back."

Charlie tipped up the last of his whiskey, "Where you headed?"

"Goddamn, Charlie. Talking to you is...is like talking to a priest!" Dash lost his patience. "Can't cha just gimme the keys and not ask a thousand questions? Can't cha?"

"I'm sorry, Dash. I'm just trying to figure out what's goin' on."

"Why? What do you need to figure out?" Dash rarely raised his voice. Never scolded the dogs, his friends or the crew. Especially never raised it to anyone he loved as much as Charlie.

Charlie acquiesced, "Alright man. Lemme go get the keys." The screen door made all the noise Charlie wished he could make. An alley mutt chased from a pail of fish heads had a more pronounced posture than Charlie did on his way through the house. He grabbed his keys off a hook by the refrigerator and another

Budweiser, intent on dampening the sting, and returned to the porch.

"Here ya go. She's full of gas."

"Thanks, Charlie." Dash held his head like it weighed a hundred pounds, and it felt off-center between his shoulders. "Look, Charlie, I'm sorry, man. It's been a real bad day, as you know...as you know, and—"

Charlie interrupted him, "Just tell me where you're goin'. You know Gary and Jules will skin me alive if they find out I let you drive off in my truck shit-faced drunk." He spoke into the glow of a lighter in the palm of his hand. "C'mon man, have a goddamn heart, Dash."

"I'm heading to Hok'ee's."

"Hok'ee's?" Charlie said, more assertive than he meant to. The humidity crackled with electricity and the rattling of armor. Charlie, the more sober of the two, resheathed his sword, and spoke in a measured voice.

"Hok'ee's, huh. That's good. You always seemed to find some peace out there. But, Dash—we're planning a service for Westie. You planning on bein' here for that?"

Dash pulled the last drag from his Marlboro and raised his sunglasses. "No, Charlie. I'm not. And I'm afraid Westie ain't gonna make it, either."

"I'm sorry, Dash. I'm a bit drunk right now and you're kinda fuckin' with my head." Charlie sat on the top step, eye level with Dash. "Can you please stop talkin' around corners and tell me..."

At that moment, Charlie froze mid-sentence. The crack was silent, but the ozone pungent as he glanced over Dash's shoulder to the Benz in the driveway. In particular, to the stiff, silhouetted figure in the front seat. Charlie wanted to believe anything but what he thought he was seeing.

"Dash, I'm gonna be real careful here. I'm gonna pick my words as best I can cause we're friends. We been friends a long time...and you're my boss. I know where my bread is buttered and all that colloquial bullshit, but...is that Westie in the front seat of your fuckin' car?"

Dash glanced back over his shoulder and drew another cigarette, "Well, Charlie. It is. That is indeed one Paul James West in the front seat of my fuckin' car." Dash turned and stumbled towards his car. There was no more mystery to the moment. Go time.

Charlie treaded lightly on the gravel in his bare feet. "How'd you? Dash...ah, shit man!"

"I stole him. I'm not gonna tell you anymore, 'cuz the more you know, the more trouble you could be in."

"Dash, is this about that crazy pact? You mean, that shit is real?" Charlie forgot himself. "Goddamn it, Dash! You've got a dead guy in your car. Soon to be in my truck!"

Dash spun to a stop at the passenger side door of the

Benz. "Calm down, Charlie." Dash wrestled Westie's stiff carcass towards Charlie's truck. "Either help me here, or shut the hell up, would ya?" Grunting, cursing under his breath, his sunglasses and hair tangled into a sweaty mess, punctuated by alcohol and cigarette smoke. West was heavy.

"Dash, I'm not that smart, but there's gotta be about five crimes going on here. Stealing a body? Driving it...cross country? Remember that whole Gram Parsons mess?"

Dash lost any remaining composure. "Goddammit, Charlie! Please...shut up! Will you shut the fuck up? I know. I remember Gram fucking Parsons. I'm well aware I have my best friend's body in your truck!" Dash stopped himself. Heady from the low atmospheric pressure swirling, he reset. "Look man. We have been friends a long time, you and me. All of us. I gotta do this for West. I don't expect you to understand."

At that moment, he jumped in the driver's seat and jammed in the key. The truck roared to life. "You'll get your truck back. You have my word." Dash slammed the door. With the window down, he thrust his elbow onto the door frame. "That's still worth sumthin', right?"

Charlie could feel the irregular edges of gravel. "What the hell am I supposed to tell Gary? Jules? What if the press finds out? The cops are gonna be lookin' for you."

"That's why I'm in your truck." Without hesitation,

Dash threw the truck into reverse, nearly crushing Charlie's bare feet. The truck lurched back in a cloud of dust. The engine revved as the tires struggled to gain traction. The glowing red taillights diminished under a sliver of a still rising moon. The tires screeched when they caught the warm tarmac and the GMC Dually swerved into the darkness.

Charlie realized it had indeed been a long day.

eight

Pristine ribbons of concrete to replace undesirable slum areas and make evacuation easier in the event of an atomic attack—that's how Dwight D. Eisenhower sold the Interstate Highway Act of 1956 to the American people. And, for what will appear as a speck on the universal time line, we bought in.

These days, St. Louis, from the highway, is indiscernible from Kansas City, Lincoln, Nebraska, or any other spot in our homogenized, imagination-less nation. *Heady thoughts for this early in the morning*, Dash thought.

The side mirrors were glowing in the morning light. The hot orange sun swelled his eyes further with their bare knuckles. The 6.6-liter turbo was well beyond thirsty and Dash was pushing it trying to get west of Oklahoma City. Past Westgate and Stone Mill. Yukon fell off to the north. The living hell known as Walmart Supercenter and its adjoining purgatories, Target and Lowe's, were far too populated to stop with a dead guy in the backseat, and so, they drifted by to the south.

Exit 132: N. Cimarron Road
Clarence E. Page Municipal Airport

The bug-smattered GMC rumbled to a stop at pump nine. Just behind A & A Tank Truck Company and across the street from Statuary World Poolside and Patio Retreats sat Love's Travel Plaza. Dash left the truck idling in park and laid his head on the leather headrest. He didn't dare close his eyes. Westie was visible in the rearview, his grey complexion peeking out from beneath the faded yellow Key West cap. Even with the AC on full bore, Westie's emanations were evident. The bacteria were invading. The mental image of a crew cab filled with airborne, flesh-eating mites caused Dash to move with purpose.

One Pack of American Spirits, light blue
One large coffee, black
One Heineken, 20-ounce
One chicken biscuit
One bottled water
Sixty-three gallons of diesel

"Anything else?" The pimply cashier was way too specific. Too chipper. Dash shook his head and handed over his credit card. His lower back cramped and shortened his strides. Once in the cockpit of the truck, his mind tripped to Hok'ee. To Jules. His cell phone. He turned it off after receiving the text from her just before going into the morgue.

The turbo was happy, churning up the acceleration lane. The black smoke disappeared quickly in the morning sky and the dead man circus was once again ripping along that glorious ribbon of concrete.

The hot coffee rested in the cup holder adjacent to the drippy Heineken in the center console. Its warm, greasy aroma, thrown off by the innocent biscuit, quickly mixed with the corpse flower and spoiled any chance at an enjoyable breakfast. Dash launched it through the passenger side window and glanced in the rearview at the disintegrating buttermilk shrapnel.

The 20-ounce would have to suffice. The cold aluminum can felt good between his legs. He fumbled through his backpack for his phone. A pleasant tone signaled its rebirth. Text message and voicemail beeps came through rapid-fire.

Dash sipped the burnt coffee.

Contacts.

Hoke.

Dash didn't know what to say when he heard Hok'ee's soft voice. "Good morning, old friend."

Dash was driving fast—too fast. "Hey Hoke. How you doing?"

"I am good my friend. Blessed. It's great to hear your voice, but you sound tired."

Dash laughed. "Yeah, Hoke...I'm tired. Listen. I just passed Oklahoma City. I'm headed your way."

"Yes? I get to see you?" Hok'ee was elated. "Is West with you?"

"Yeah, he's with me." Dash gulped his Heineken. "But Hoke—Westie's gone. He died. Yesterday."

Dash could hear Hok'ee breathing.

"I'm sorry Dash. I'm sorry you lost..." Hok'ee's voice was choked and broken, "We lost our dear friend. I'll make sure things are as they need to be for your arrival."

All Dash could muster was a thanks. His eyes were filling. He was losing the stitches on the ribbon. Hok'ee had something else to say.

"You know, Dash, my heart has been resisting this day for many years. I feared for the one who was left. I prayed that I might pass before I had to witness the fissure. And now—my heart breaks for you."

The line went dead.

Dash hadn't been paying attention to the road. The car sped up from behind so fast, he thought it was, for sure, in hot pursuit of an offender up ahead. Not so. Lights were flashing. The trooper blasted the siren in short bursts. He got so close, the strobing headlights on the Impala disappeared below the tailgate of the truck.

Adrenaline smacked Dash sober. His brain was firing, searching for the threads of a lie to explain the dead guy in the back seat. *Get rid of the beer.*

The center console on Charlie's truck was big enough to house a small family of gypsies. He quickly stowed the half-empty can and covered it with his backpack. Chugging a mouthful of burnt coffee, he lit a cigarette and pulled to the shoulder.

"Holy fuckin' shit man...keep it together."

He could see the young cop talking into his radio. The soft leather wrap on the wheel would absorb the moisture from his gushing pores for only so long. Dash pulled his sunglasses down. A vain attempt. Slow and steady, the officer approached the window, right hand resting on his sidearm. There was no way he was gonna miss the corpse flower.

"Morning, sir." He said. "License and registration, please."

Dash puffed so fast and hard on the cigarette, he created a headspin. Dizzy from the lack of oxygen, he fought the restraint of the seatbelt, and stretched for the registration in the glove box, which might as well have been a mile away.

"Here you go."

"William-Henry Nelson. Well, I'll be goddamned. That is your real name."

Dash was half buzzed, dead tired, and thoroughly confused.

"Excuse me officer, but it's Dash. Just...Dash."

The young officer pulled off his aviators and stared Dash straight in the face.

"Do you know how fast you were going Mr. Nelson?"

"No sir, I don't." The less said, the better.

"Ninety-five miles an hour. Ninety-five!"

"That's awful fast."

"Yes sir, it is. Can you please step out of the truck? And...uh, I'm gonna need you to wake your passenger."

Dash opened the door, knowing full well he was probably going to jail. He began checking his pockets. For what, he wasn't quite sure. It just happened whenever he got nervous. He pushed his sunglasses to the top of his head, immediately regretting it.

"Mr. Nelson..."

"Please—it's Dash." The officers suspicion was blinded and completely brushed aside by his admiration for Mr. Dash Nelson. He handed Dash his license saying, "This is a nice truck you got here."

"Thanks, it's not mine. It's belongs to my tour manager."

"Can you tell me who that might be sir?" The officer was standing as officers do, with his hands on his hips, accusatory and all.

"Well sure. That'd be Charlie Tate."

"Okay, Dash. I gotcha."

Dash's silence left the window open for the officer to expand on just what "I gotcha" meant.

"Today is your lucky day." The officer said with a tight-lipped smile.

Dash had to chuckle at the irony. The officer didn't appreciate the humor. "I'm sorry," he said, "Did I say something funny?" Dash shook his head.

"I'm a big, big fan. In fact, I got your album 'Across State Lines' on my phone right here. Listen." That he did. Right there, on the shoulder of the interstate, his tiny phone squeezed out the low-fi title track. And, at that precise moment, Dash was wishing the kind officer would have just taken him straight to jail.

"C'mon Dash, sing some of it for me," the officer said extending his arm high above them both, as if a loud speaker was blasting John Phillips Souza.

"Honestly, it's a little early," Dash said. "I'm no good before noon."

"Well, sir. Alright. I understand. I've caught you off guard." The officer's features were that of a new college graduate. His crew cut attempted to add some age, but it only served to expose a chin that resembled the soft pink balls of a young bull.

"I'm not gonna cite you today, sir. I do, however, need to you wake your passenger. I need to see his ID."

Ah, Jesus Christ, Dash thought. *There ain't no ID! No shoes, either.*

"Officer, Westie's dead tired. And if I may be totally

honest, a bit hungover. We've been driving all night. I've been...I've been driving all night. I sure hate to wake him for this."

"That's Westie back there?" The young officer might have pissed his khaki trousers at the news. "Hell, he's a living legend. I'm sorry, I need a photo with you two. I know it's against the rules, professional protocol and what have you, but—I can't not get a photo. My wife'll kill me."

"Okay." Dash was exasperated. There was nothing to do but play along. Dash banged on the back door and danced front and center in the highway dog and pony show.

"West! C'mon man...get up. Officer wants a picture. Selfie time." He opened the door and patted Westie's stiff, rigamortis-ridden leg, almost vomiting in his mouth. "Hey! Officer wants a picture. Get up, you old pecker head!" Officer Martin peered over Dash's shoulder. Dash employed a small boxing out maneuver to keep him at nose length.

"Officer, I'm sorry man, but he's dead to the world. When Westie gets like this, there's no wakin' him. I'm afraid, I'm gonna have to be your trophy bass."

After what seemed like two-dozen asinine photos that were almost certain to get the young man relieved of his duty should he not resist the urge to post them on whatever God-forsaken social media page he subscribed to, Dash astoundingly found himself stomping the accelerator; pulling off the shoulder of the road.

No ticket, no arrest, and questioning the competence of mankind. The earth's rotation seemed to stumble on a piece of small gravel. A hiccup in the pocket of Minkowski's continuum actually allowed that man to become an officer of the law.

It was then Dash remembered the Heineken in the center console.

nine

Charlie stood on the front porch, sipping his coffee. He'd done a lot of that lately—standing on the porch—when he saw the white Range Rover turn into his driveway. He hadn't even had a chance to finish the first cup before he realized he was going to need something much stronger for this discussion. Before Jules reached the house, he went to the kitchen and put on a fresh pot. He re-emerged just as the Rover came to rest next to Dash's 560.

Jules Elizabeth Nelson was forty-three. A New York City girl turned L.A. hippie. Her father was an English professor at Fordham. Her mother, named poet laureate in 1994, visited the White House at the request of Mr. Bill Clinton.

Jules' apple didn't fall far from the tree, but it rolled

a bit once it landed. Her bohemian mien engaged in regular skirmishes with her supermodel exterior. Further complicating the matter of pigeon-holing a beautiful woman was her brain. She had one. And it was incredibly well-stocked and scalpel-sharp.

Long bangs playing hide and seek with jade green eyes and seemed to tiptoe across her eyelashes when she blinked. The rest of her chocolate mane hung straight, like silk curtains, coming to rest on the gentle slope of her round breasts, all just a tad bit north of where long stems meet perfect hips.

With a Fordham BA in Fine Arts complete, daddy was happy. Jules flew to Los Angeles for a modeling job. An escape from New York. The money was just too good to pass up. She said, after it was all over, at no other time in her life had she ever imagined that fifteen-hundred dollar shoes could make her feel like such a whore.

On the positive side, the check cleared. And Jules met Mickey Kelly, the photographer who shot the layout. Mickey was an addict the second he caught whiff of her, and for Jules, Mickey was as good a reason as any to stay in L.A.

Dash's orbit collided with Jules' stardust when Mickey got hired to shoot the cover for a Rolling Stone expose. Dash, Mickey and Jules spent two complicated days in Taos, New Mexico. Dash would later admit, like Mickey, he was ruined the moment he met her.

Twenty-two months can be a lifetime and it can be instant. Jules wasn't sure on which end of the spectrum she sat, but that's how long their circles overlapped. She pondered that very sentiment as she watched Mickey's coffin make the descent into a small hole in West Hollywood. There wasn't much Mickey left after he crashed his Ducati on the Pacific Coast Highway. Jules closed shop. She felt a little like a dying dolphin, her colors fading into that of galvanized chain. She took what Mickey taught her and split to Africa, then Europe.

As fate would have it, Dash was finishing up a European run of dates, the last being in London. Jules was scheduled to fly out of Heathrow airport the afternoon of his show but there was a pile-up at the corner of Kismet and Providence, and her flight got canceled. While checking into the Regent Hotel, she happened past a poster, "DASH NELSON: BARBICAN HALL." The date was that night. Jules showed up at the backstage door, camera in hand. That was the excuse. Professional interest. Strictly business. She missed every other flight out of Heathrow.

Charlie had an extra cup of coffee in his hand. He tried to stop the screen door from slamming by trailing his bare foot, but his timing was off. Jules strode up to the porch; jeans, cowboy boots and a crisp white V-neck tee.

"Morning, Charlie. Where is he?"

"He's not here, Jules," Charlie said, extending the cup to Jules.

"What do you mean he's not here? Where could he be?" She set the coffee on the porch rail without so much as tasting its steam. "His car's right there. Don't make me beg, Charlie."

"Jules, you know I can't lie to you."

"Charlie, you can't lie to anyone." They both chuckled. Jules continued, "Look, this is getting outta hand. Apparently, Dash stole Westie's body from the morgue last night. Did you know that, Charlie?" Jules stared into Charlie face.

"I know that now, yes."

"Okay good. So he was here." Jules's bangs were tiptoeing. "Did he really have Westie with him?"

Charlie, raising his eyebrows, said, "Jules, you need to grab that coffee and come inside. We need to talk." Her face went blank.

"Charlie, you're scaring me. The police are looking for Dash. He could be in a lot of trouble. What the hell was he thinking?"

Charlie held the screen door with his body. Glancing at the ground, he held out his arm inviting her into the house. "I'm gonna tell ya what he was thinking. But you certainly ain't gonna like it."

ten

Gary's assistant buzzed through, "Gary, I have Charlie on the line, can you take it?"

"Sure Kelly, thanks. Hello, Charlie. How ya doin'?"

Charlie was tense. "Not too good Gary. Not too good."

"I know Charlie, it's been a crazy couple of days. You heard from Dash?"

"No. But I have heard from Jules. She's been here all morning. Now the police are calling. They know he's got my truck. I couldn't lie Gary, I'm sorry."

"Charlie, don't apologize. Nobody expects you to lie. Listen, I don't wanna discuss this on the phone. It's 11:30, meet me at Bobby's for lunch, noon. I'm buying. We'll talk then."

"Okay," Charlie said. "I'll see ya at Bobby's."

Gary grabbed his sport coat from the back of his

chair, his steps slowed slightly but never completely stopped on the way past. "Kelly, I gotta run out for a bit, that gonna mess up my afternoon?"

"Nope. You're good. You have a two-o'clock, you need me to move it?"

"No. I'll be back by one. I'll have the cell."

Gary's silver 550 swung into the gravel lot just before noon. Charlie looked as if he were trying to screw himself into the ground. Feet crossed, arms folded, leaning heavy on the front fender of Dash's car.

"Hey Charlie."

"Hey Gar."

"I would've been happy to come get you."

"It's fine. This just ain't no fun." Charlie was glum. "First, Jules gave me the third degree, then the cops, and now, I gotta drive this piece-a-shit with dead Westie funk all over it. I don't wanna go to jail, Gar."

"Okay, Charlie. Let's go inside, grab a beer. You're not going to jail. You haven't done anything wrong."

"Aidin' and abetting? You consider that nuthin'?"

"C'mon Charlie. You need a drink. I'll tell ya what I know."

Most of Music Row's history had been long done in. Bowled over. Fragments buried under ever-antiquating studios, publishing houses and non-penitent, phallic condominiums. Bobby's cinder-block bomb shelter appeal stood in stark contrast, thumbing its long-paid-for nose at the developmental establishment.

Gary and Charlie got their usual seat in the corner booth by the front window. Gary tried to ease Charlie's mind.

"All morning long, I've been researching and talking to folks about this whole situation. I've been getting calls from my attorney friends, trial lawyers, tax lawyers, prosecutors and few of my pals at Metro."

After ordering, Gary waited for the waitress to leave before he continued. "Now, here's the deal, Charlie. You didn't aid or abet anything. There has to be a crime before you can aid or abet. And...there was no crime."

"Gary, he stole a damn body!"

Gary hushed him with a hand gesture. "Listen to me for a second, will ya? That's not technically a crime. I know it's crazy, but here's how it shakes out. The kid, the coroner's assistant, what's his name...Christian? He let Dash into the morgue, so there's no trespassing charge. The body was not involved in a homicide, so there's no obstruction of justice. Dash broke the window, allegedly...that amounts to a possible vandalism charge. That's a misdemeanor. Hell, the morgue is worried we're gonna sue them for negligence!"

The waitress's return and departure was swift. Budweiser for Charlie and a Manhattan for Gary. Charlie eyed her, waiting to speak. "Are you kidding me? You can steal a body and it's not a crime?"

Gary sipped his Manhattan. "Well, if the body was buried, we might have a problem. But thanks to good ole Lord Coke, who declared, under common law, 'a corpse has no value'." Gary smiled at his research. "See: Collins v New York Organ Donor Society, Inc., two-thousand-and-six, section 8 N.Y.3d 43, pages...fifty and fifty-one." Gary winked, raised his glass, and slurped intentionally.

Charlie smiled cautiously, "Who the hell is Lord Coke?"

Gary waved his hand and laughed, "Don't worry about it. He's been dead for almost half a century."

Charlie tipped his beer and swigged mightily. "Well that's good news, Gar. Now I gotta ask, what about the pact? What about tor..."

Gary interrupted, "Stop! I don't know nuthin' about no pact. I'm not privy to that information, and dang it, Charlie, I don't wanna be. Whatever you know, don't tell me. Don't say another word. I can't unhear it and I'm not gonna get wrapped up in the crazy shit Dash and Westie seem to attract like flies."

Gary's complexion began to rival the maraschino cherry in his quickly disappearing glass. "I got too many years in this wagon. I ain't about to see it toppled by some fantastical Hollywood bullshit." His wide Kentucky jaw flexed. Through clenched teeth, Gary said, "Let's talk about sumthin' else. I wanna enjoy this drink before I gotta go back to my office.

Neither of them noticed the impeccably dressed man approaching the table. The tailored grey suit, light blue tie and Italian shoes should have been as obvious as a bright red fire truck screaming down a dirt lane. Hell, the last time Bobby's saw someone in a suit was in 1972 when Elvis spent two nights at the Ryman.

"Gentlemen, I'm sorry to interrupt." Gary and Charlie, neither a fan of surprises, were both...caught by surprise. "I'm special agent Watts, FBI, Memphis Division. Is this a bad time?" Charlie nearly choked at the ID badge thrust into their faces. Gary was as smooth as crushed velvet, sliding out of the booth, completely ignoring Watts' attempt to intimidate.

"Well, Agent Watts, it is a bad time. Let's go Charlie, we've got that meeting to get to." Charlie quickly stood up, nodded at Watts, brushing his shoulder as he passed. "Scuze me, sir."

Gary tossed a twenty on the table. Buttoning his jacket, he, too, nodded his salutation, "Agent Watts."

With strands of pork fat clinging to his rear molars, and halitosis of sweet barbecue, Watts said, "Gentlemen, I'm gonna need to speak with you at some point in time. Putting me off isn't going to help Mr. Nelson."

Gary turned, with his hands in his pockets, and in his best, unassuming lawyer voice said, "Agent Watts... there's been no crime. Mr. Nelson needs no help. I'm afraid you've wasted your time."

Gary's perfect Hollywood exit was all but spoiled when Watts fired back, "Well, Mr. Smith...some people, especially folks in this town, don't seem to think three-hundred-thousand dollars is a lot of money. The FBI thinks differently."

eleven

When Dash made the turn off Route 191 onto Indian Rte. 7, he felt the collision with his exhaustion. The thumbnail sliver of a moon did little to illuminate the oxidized steel letters hovering high in mid-air over Hok'ee's gate. MA'IITSOH SIN.

"The wolf song," Dash muttered to himself as he leaned forward into the windshield to watch it pass overhead.

The sky went on forever. Eggplant purple, draped like silk. Buttes—sentries at attention—standing watch over coyote, hawk and sage. The high beams punched at the darkness. The dashboard hue uplit Dash's face so strangely it startled him when he caught his own likeness in the rearview. The bacterial stench was pungent now. The truck ghosted to a halt.

Hok'ee was standing barefoot and bare-chested in

the dirt. His long salt and pepper braids hung straight and tight to just above his nipples. A bone buffalo-hair pipe breastplate adorned with feathers and bronze beads hung in between. His wrists cuffed in sterling and turquoise. Two thick silver rings, one on each forefinger. Black jeans made his torso look as though it was mounted on an ebony wedge. Turlo, his massive Pyrenees mountain dog sat motionless at his side, a contrast in stark white fur, eyes glowing like Baltic amber.

Dash left the engine running and the AC on full blast as he stretched himself upright, hands at his hips, desperately trying to release the tension in his lower back and legs. Hok'ee whispered something under his breath, releasing Turlo from his side. The cloud trotted to Dash, tail wagging, tongue dripping with spit, wet greetings.

Dash squatted. "Hey buddy...who's a good boy?" He rubbed Turlo's square head and tousled his ears. Wincing as he stood, he walked to greet Hok'ee, who hadn't moved an inch or uttered a word.

"Hello, you old dog," Dash said as the two embraced.

Hok'ee patted Dash on the back slowly like a mother to a son. "Hello my friend. Welcome back."

When they separated, Hok'ee took several steps towards the running truck, stopped and turned toward Dash with a look not yet seen in their long friendship.

Hok'ee Binali was once Terrance Banally, the critically-acclaimed and highly sought-after Renaissance Man. A musician, poet and painter, Hok'ee had been a victim of the atrocities of the 50s and 60s when white Americans decided that breaking up Native American families was a good idea. Hok'ee had been taken from his parents, under the auspices of the United States Government on trumped up, bogus charges. They shipped him off to LA and branded him with a new name. Terrance.

The City of Angels foster system did a great disservice to the young Native American wrapped in the candy shell of a white man. Finally, on his 18th birthday, bound for the anonymity of New York City's avenues, he stuck his thumb out on the entrance ramp to I-10.

A few months living in a van on St. Marks Place can change anyone's perspective. January in the city is a bitch. Flea bites looked like needle tracks. Everybody was avant-garde in those days. To be truly avant-garde, the counter culture looked almost normal, but with a small birth defect here and there. A tick.

Terrance's particular brand of twitch was as regular on the art scene as pigeon shit and turpentine. Although a man can drown lying face up on solid rock if it rains hard enough, there is always the narcotizing possibility his luck can change.

And...one day, his luck did change. The day when

Andy Warhol and Gerard Melanga decided to start a small magazine called *Interview*. Terrance got a tip that Andy might want to do a feature on his music, his poetry. His 'trip" as Andy put it.

Warhol had been managing the Velvet Underground at the time, and felt Lou and Terrance needed to meet. Terry, as Andy called him, was causing quite the stir. The penultimate, a famous photo that catapulted his stature on the New York scene, featured a glassy-eyed Terrance staring directly into the lens, getting kissed by Lou Reed. A joint in one hand, a cocktail napkin in the other that read, "Fuck Pizza! Eat Pussy."

Terrance was in. Hip. Dangerous and out of control. There was no peace with his white man name, and now—it was all over him. *Interview Magazine* published the article along with the highly controversial photo of Terry and Lou.

The article ended with this quote from Terrance: "I'm not who you think I am. I'm an actor. Just like all of you. I'm improvising, shooting from the hip. It's all a lie. I'm a lie. You're a lie. The lights—they don't lie. But when they shine, they only tell half the story."

Terrance was sucked into the rabbit hole. And it drove him nuts. In 1985, Terrance was in Nashville of all places, attending a birthday party for the clothing designer Miguel. Dash and West were at the same party. Amoebas, the three instantly became one. Terrance's words and music were interlaced throughout Dash's *Across State Lines* record.

When Andy died unexpectedly in 1987, Terrance sailed off into a fog that didn't burn off for nearly a decade. When it did, on a fateful day in 1995, the skies were anything but clear, and Terry attempted the ultimate self-betrayal.

Sometimes when you fail, you actually succeed. A message not lost on Terry. With his second chance clenched firmly in his fist, he began his rebirth. He rejected the name given by the government agents, and the trappings that went with it. He shut out the pop-culture world, disavowed his past, and threw himself head first into the kiln of a new life.

He peeled the shell, losing both flesh and nail. On his new ranch, on the fringe of the Navajo reservation, he reclaimed his Navajo birth name, Hok'ee Binali, the high-backed wolf.

Two silver rings.
One for the life once lived.
One for the life yet lived.

"Dash," Hok'ee said, still a few feet from the truck, "the Navajo have very strong traditions surrounding the dead." Dash listened to his friend. "I'm split like the oak from lightning. One half loves you and my brother West. The other half loves my tradition. My faith. You've come here for peace, yet you bring me great trouble."

Dash was dumbfounded, "Hoke...I didn't mean..."

He was interrupted, "I know you mean me no harm. We've been brothers a long time. We walked through the flames together in our youth, but I'm old now. The spirits will punish me for this...this pact we made as misguided souls. I am now supposed to honor the words of dead men."

Dash walked to meet Hok'ee who held up a hand to stop him. "Dash, please...I must make peace with this. Do you know about Navajo beliefs? Do you know about the dead's spirit returning to punish the living?"

"Hoke, I'm sorry. This thing's got me twisted, too. It's been a long couple of days. I'm about to fall out. Westie, he's...he's ripe—like, well, like he's been dead for two days. I need some help here."

Hok'ee said, "Let's get him out of that truck." Dash bowed his head in both relief and exhaustion. "But we can't bring him into the house. If we are to carry on with this foolishness, it will be done in the barn."

Dash patted Hok'ee on the shoulder, wincing at the odor coming out of the truck as he opened the doors, "I'm sure he's gonna be fine with that."

twelve

Few things provoke the olfactory as do the desert at night and horse manure. Whitethorn acacia and sweetbush mixed with the kicked-up scent of fresh straw as Hok'ee and Dash shuffled into the barn. As gently as possible, they set Westie on a makeshift table Hok'ee had fashioned with a couple of saw horses and a sheet of four-by-eight.

"The dead will return to the living." Hok'ee was winded. "I built this house, this ranch with the only life I have left. I can't lose it at this age."

"Hoke...West ain't comin' back to punish you. He would never do that. Right now, far as I can tell, he's on a fifty-foot sloop with six chicks and bottle of tequila. Shit, the last thing you gotta worry about is Westie's spirit."

Hok'ee wiped the sweat from his forehead, and

allowed a chuckle to escape. Then Hok'ee's smile faded. "You have a difficult day ahead of you. Let's go to the house. I'll make some tea. We need to talk about what's going to happen.

Turlo spiraled himself before dropping down to the cool kitchen tile in front of the sink. Hok'ee put on a kettle of water and pulled down two small glasses from the cupboard. The clanking of glassware, silverware and cabinet drawers was the vehicle of conversation for the moment. With the soft blue flames doing their work, Hok'ee joined Dash at the table with two stout pours of fine tequila along with the bottle.

The smiles were forced. The tequila was smooth. Easy. It served to dilate the discussion. Dash threw out the first pitch. A high, fast curve-ball.

"Why'd you do it, Hoke?"

There was no flinch. No uneasiness. It was a question Hok'ee had been expecting for the last twenty years. He spun his tequila with a thumb and middle finger. Eyed it like a stack of chips and he was contemplating the busted flush.

"You know—every day, I see free men searching for a cage to ease them of their burden. I was in prison when we met. But I invented my cage. Built it, one bar at a time. I wanted to stop lying to myself. When Andy died, it looked like freedom to me. I took a handful of freedom."

Dash nodded, "I'm sorry, Hoke."

The analog whistle of steam sent Hok'ee to the stove. He returned with two glazed mugs of his own creation and some honey.

"It's my turn." Hok'ee poured more tequila. "Why'd you let her go?"

"Well, your honor..." Dash smirked. "When one tree burns, the whole forest is at risk of burning. Jules didn't need to be so close to the flames."

"Interesting choice of words, my friend. She's the best thing that's ever happened to you. You know that, right?"

"Yeah. I know it."

"We should get to the business at hand."

Dash wiped a thumb across the face of his watch. "Whaddaya say we hit the porch. I need to reinforce a bad habit."

The two men gathered their tea, tequila and, with Turlo leading the parade, resigned to the porch. Dash stood and pissed through the balusters, squinting as blue smoke assaulted his right eye.

"Let's talk about this pact," Hok'ee started.

"You know the pact, Hoke. What's to talk about?"

"I know that Westie had a fascination with the Native Americans. I know he wanted a Navajo ceremony because I was Navajo. Westie wanted to be Navajo. But...Westie wasn't Navajo, Dash. He was an Irish kid from New Jersey who grew up to become a maker. He made people into other people. He facilitated dreams. Your dreams. He was a brother, but he was no Navajo."

"So...what are you sayin' here, Hoke?"

Hok'ee was staring ahead. "I'm saying this is crazy. We were foolish. I should have known better. But—drugs, they fuck you up. I should have never agreed. To carry on with this is reckless."

Dash leaned across the small table between them, almost burning a hole in side of Hok'ee's face with his glance. "Hoke—you and I both know this is much more complicated than some cavalier pact."

Hok'ee confirmed as much with deafening silence. "Listen," Dash said. "Just tell me what I gotta do, and I'll be outta your hair. I want this to end as much as you, Hoke."

"First we must cleanse the body. Navajo customs are very strict about this. Once Westie is clean, he is to be wrapped. We will use the burial blanket I had made for my ceremony."

"Hoke, you can't do that." Dash protested.

Hok'ee heard none of it. "Bleeding Rock is a good day's ride from here. You'll take the buckskin, Shaman. My young paint will go with West. Blink is a smart, strong pony. He'll serve him well."

"I'm lost, Hoke. What do you mean, the paint pony goes with West?"

Hok'ee poured more tequila. "Dash, once you're done with West, you must kill the pony. You must bury it alongside his body."

Dash stood up too fast. "What?! Are you nuts? I gotta kill the horse! Hok'ee. I'm a singer. Besides my marriage, I haven't killed anything in my whole goddamn life. I can't kill a horse."

Hok'ee smirked remorsefully. "This is not a negotiation. This is the ceremony. The horse is for Westie to ride in the afterlife. It must be young. It must be strong. The pony is...all of that." Hok'ee poured himself a measure of tequila and drank it quickly, fighting the welling of water in his eyes. Dash was silent.

Hok'ee said, "You remember what happened with Gram, right?"

"Gram? Of course I remember what happened with Gram. Phil poured a five-gallon jug of gas into his coffin and lit a match. The damn thing nearly blew his head off."

"Right," Hok'ee said. "And the body didn't burn. That's because it takes 2000 degrees for many hours to burn a body to ashes. You can't make a fire that hot with sticks in the desert."

The reality was upon Dash. "So how do I get this done Hoke?"

"Thermite."

"Okay. Thermite. What the hell is it and how do I get it?"

"Thermite is iron oxide mixed with aluminum

powder. It burns at two-thousand degrees...Celsius. Dangerous is an understatement." Dash was paying close attention.

"Iron oxide? Rust? You make this stuff with rust?"

"Rust and aluminum. It'll burn clean through an engine block."

"How'my gonna carry this stuff? How do I light it?"

"We'll separate the ingredients until it's time to mix them. When you arrive at the site, you must dig a ditch deep enough to hide the flash. It will be seen for miles. You must not look at it! The flash is as bright as the sun. It'll blind you. Next, you'll fill small terracotta pots with the powder and set em in the ditch. Build, with stacked sticks an altar, on which to set Westie. This can all be ignited with a simple fuse."

Dash knew that when contemplating death, a man, being of sound mind and body, should see to it that he doesn't further complicate matters by mixing in large quantities of tequila and volatile explosive ingredients.

"I'm gonna need more tequila, Hoke."

"Wait until I tell you to get naked."

thirteen

Whatever was left of the waxing crescent was not visible from the ranch. It was time to tend to West. On their way to the barn, Hok'ee stopped at a smoldering fire pit to stoke the coals and add fuel. Two galvanized buckets of water faced off atop the rusting metal grate that rested its edges on the stone perimeter.

In that imperceptible moment when Dash broke the plane of the barn doors, any resolution he might have imagined he had about the evening's events vanished. There lay Westie in his ridiculous outfit. Earlier, Dash had taken great pains to get the Key West hat to stay on Westie's head. Seemed important at the time.

The smolder quickly ignited the dry mesquite. High flames cast long shadows into the barn. Old bourbon barrels, forcibly removed from their rings in the dirt, were re-purposed through imminent domain as tables to hold the oil lanterns and candles. Both, at any other time, forbidden in a half-century-old wooden barn full of hay and straw; tonight, their natural energy lit the place up like St. Peter's Basilica.

Hok'ee snatched a well-worn feed scoop and gathered a mound of ashes from the pit. Warm to the touch, he set it to cool on a barrel next to two pairs of tattered moccasins and a small glass vial. Neither man, with their current alcohol content, needed to pass too closely to any open flames.

"Okay, my friend. Remove your clothes." Hok'ee said, starting to undress.

"Everything?"

Hok'ee, for the first time in decades, removed the two silver rings from his fingers, pausing at the significance. The two men stood, one on each side of Westie, naked. Flaccid; children grown old.

"Put these on." Hok'ee said, handing over a pair of moccasins. An arduous task in the current state of inebriation. "Cup your hands." Hok'ee filled Dash's hands with ashes, then his own. Dash stood, arms extended, unsure of what to do next. Hok'ee began rubbing the ashes into his face and neck. Shoulders, arms, chest... everything. Head to toe. Hok'ee's eyes shined white like dinner plates, his body black from top to bottom.

"The ash protects us from the evil spirits."

Dash's eyes were wide with a rising terror when he

began the same ritual, rubbing, spitting the ash from his lips, dipping into the warm metal scoop again and again, until he was covered in warm, black ash.

He followed Hok'ee's smeared, leathered ass to the fire pit where each gathered a bucket of steaming water. Back at the table, Hok'ee poured a measure from the vial, into each pail. He lit a small bundle, and with Dash's help, undressed West.

And, in the spirals of sage smoke, with the scent of death deep in their synapse, they silently, lovingly, set about the task of washing their dead friend's body.

fourteen

Dash fingered his ear, not quite satisfied he'd remembered every orifice from which ash had to be scrubbed. To the voyeur with fogged-up binoculars in some imaginary trailer, straining its axles on deflated tires in an imaginary trailer park, Dash in the shower that particular evening resembled d'Artagnan in a duel with a cobweb.

***

From the saddle, he wondered whether he could remember all that he needed to remember. Shaman drew a deep breath, expanding the girth strap. Dash took a quick visual inventory, finishing on a pair of saddle bags across Shaman's quarters. Thermite ingredients, Colt revolver, hand-held GPS, first-aid kit, and fifth of tequila. Saddle strings on the rear jockey secured a bedroll and two shovels. Forward, twin wool-covered canteens hung from the horn.

Westie's body, wrapped in Hok'ee's ceremonial blanket, was lashed athwart across the young paint, along with a second set of bags containing sweet-feed, a grain for the horses, a chunk of bread, cured meats, and an extra bladder of water.

Hok'ee was in full regalia; braids, black jeans, turquoise cuffs, breast plate and silver rings.

"It's a full day's ride to Bleeding Rock. The reservoir is close if you need water." Stalling, he straightened the forelock between Shaman's ears.

"These horses have never been through the work you're putting on them today. Be gentle. Feed the grain only after they've cooled down. Find roughage if you can."

"I know, Hoke. We talked about this. I'll water the horses at the reservoir, and—I'll be easy on 'em. Thermite's okay in those canvas sacks?"

"Yes. Mix them on site, in the pots. Don't look at the flash flame when it ignites."

"Don't look at the flash flame…I know, Hoke. The GPS has the coordinates for Bleeding Rock?"

"You won't need them. If you follow the compass heading I gave you, the rock will find you. Remember, don't pass the bluff. You'll be off the reservation."

"Okay…I gotta go."

Hok'ee walked to Westie, placed his hands on the body and bowed his head. He chanted something in Navajo; Dash couldn't hear. When finished, Hok'ee put his head to the young paint pony's head. Softly patting Blink's neck, he whispered, again in his native language. Then he said, in English, "Take care of Westie."

Dash's eyes welled. He pretended not to hear. Hok'ee walked to Shaman. With tears in his eyes, he extended his hand, "God speed, my friend." Dash took his hand and cracked a tight smile. Hok'ee didn't linger. He pulled from Dash's grasp and walked slowly to the house, never turning back.

Dash set off, Blink and Westie in tow. He needed to make the roughly twenty-mile distance before dusk. "Okay, West. We're on our way buddy." His thoughts sprinted far ahead. Everything that had come before ricocheted off everything yet to come, constantly replaying the impossible movie of the events yet to transpire. Marching, single file, questioning God, and burning from the inside out.

Dash's torso rocked in rhythm with Shaman's soft gait. The suede gus, streaked with salt stains, kept his face in the shade. The horse blanket poncho lasted a scant few minutes before it was tucked in the lashings of the bedroll. Dash's jeans soaked through at the inner thighs from Shaman's body heat. Rivulets from the knee, not shanghaied, found their way into his boots.

Tiny clouds of dirt dust rose, then quickly drifted off like smoke rings with each of the horses' steps. Shaman's metal shoes silently measured the miles until he'd clip a small rock and stumble, Dash softly tugging the reins to keep his head up. Every so often, Dash turned side saddle to look back at the heap extending from either side of Blink's proud head.

"I'm not sure what we were thinking, West. Hok'ee was right. We were fools. Still are. Jules is ready to kill me, I promise you that. Feels like a month. You know Charlie's about lost his mind over that truck." Dash lit a cigarette, licked his fingers to snuff out the smoldering sulfur match. No brush fires today.

"Gary...Mr. Methodical. The Legal Eagle...he's probably got half the city buttoned down. You? You're the lucky one here. You don't have to explain any of this shit."

Dash pulled swig of warm water from a canteen. He remembered Hok'ee not turning back to watch him leave. He fixated on killing the pony, instantly swatting the thought from his mind. He sat forward, squinting at the horizon, questioning everything in his life to that point. "West, you're not a Navajo. You're—an Irish kid from New Jersey. What the fuck am I doing?"

***

Dash reached Bleeding Rock just before dark. Dizzy with exhaustion, occupying a space somewhere between serial killer and hallucinatory doper wandering the streets of the East Village, he dismounted Shaman. Lead legs with no structural integrity, he blinked, trying to pull focus on the angles buzzing the tower.

The monolithic, sandstone formation, narrow at its base, shot up eighty feet. It rested atop a small mountain of soil, once a part of the rock itself, now resigned to gaze up like Dash—and the rest of humanity—from below.

"Westie...I sure hope you can see this from where you are," Dash said, wiping sweat and dirt from his eyes. A million years' worth of secrets, jutting out in jagged, misaligned layers, stacked like platters after a grand ballroom dinner. Gold. Amber. The Mongolian Layer stripped naked to the sky. Raped by the wind. Eclipsed by Bierstadt's Yosemite. Crime.

One deep red, rusty stain, beginning at the top, seeped down to its base, as if an invisible dagger fell from the heavens and pierced its head, just behind the ear. Rust. The same rust Dash had in his saddle bag.

fifteen

A few miles past Bleeding Rock were the visible bluffs of Round Rock, and the edge of the reservation. Nothing sovereign past that point. Jurisdictions come into full focus out there.

He found a flat rise on which to rest and water the horses. Ironwoods and yucca lined what looked to be an arroyo just below. Enough wood to build a small cabin collected in the bows of a long-dead mesquite tree that obviously lost its grip in the torrents of water.

Shaman and Blink were shimmering with sweat in the places where blankets and breast collars rested on their taut hides. Tobosa and grama grew plentiful. The horses busied themselves refueling their furnaces. Their withers twitched. Nostrils flared with low grumbles when Dash pulled the sweet feed from the saddle bag.

The only evidence that proved this place was now a campsite was the two saddles resting on their pommels. Their undersides might have a chance to dry before morning. Westie's body lay between them, Dash's hat rested on Westie's chest.

He gathered enough wood to start a small fire, devoured the chunk of bread, along with a canteen of water, and half of the tequila. After standing for too long in the glow of the flames, he removed his shirt and started digging. Stabbing hard and deep, shovels full of soft, red earth were catapulted into the night.

Every man should have to dig his own grave, Dash thought. If for nothing else, than to know what it feels like to dig his own grave. Exhaling, drenched with sweat and streaked with dirt, he fought battles in his brain. Every battle ever waged. He retraced the routes, tore open the wounds, and took it out on the dirt. A monster slashed and tore at the dirt and began to sing *Iron Hands*, the song he had refused to sing on the highway:

> *Some days the weather is against you*
> *Some days the dirt might fight you too*
> *But when your help up and fails*
> *Your hands can feel the nails*
> *As they reach for you*

Breathing, as if to blow out the fires of hell. Sweat

puddled in the mud. Dash crawled from the hip-deep pit. Jeans stained red, damp with the blood of the desert. A murderous fiend in the glow of the fire, he pulled from the agave nectar, stabbed the cork and tossed it into the dirt.

"West!" His shout spooked the horses. "There comes a point in every man's life where the wheat and the grass dry up, and there's nothing left but the mud." Staggering, he brandished the shovel like a saber. The eyes of Shaman and Blink showed white. Fear-flared nostrils, flank to flank, rearing back, straining their halters.

"One down and one to go." Dash began a fresh hole, two to three yards east of West's hole. With the same ferociousness, he dug a bigger, deeper hole.

"Blink buddy, I'm sorry. I had no fuckin' idea West would need a horse to ride in the afterlife. The son-of-a-bitch barely rode a bicycle. What...the hell...is he gonna do with a goddamn horse."

Two days' worth of falling through the tissues of a perceived reality ended abruptly. It ain't the fall that kills you. It's the sudden stop.

In an ever-accelerating state of insobriety, Dash staggered and lost his balance. To stop himself from falling, he let go of the shovel, which sent the load of dirt streaming into his face. Spitting wildly, hysterically shaking his head, trying to absterge the dirt from his burning eyes, Dash stomped on the blade of the shovel, which blasted the shaft upwards and squarely into his left testicle.

He lost all will to remain upright and fell flat on his back in the pit. Gazing at the stars, real and imaginary, he ventured, "A—goddamn—horse? Holy mother of God...my fuckin' balls."

Dash craned himself up onto his knees, wincing, blinking profusely. Unable to see anything with any nocturnal clarity, he scampered to the canteen. Dousing his face, spreading the red mud down his chest, he choked on his breath. Grabbing the denim shirt he jettisoned earlier, he managed to wipe clear his eyes. In the glow of the dying fire, Blink and Shaman stood motionless, shoulder to shoulder, muzzles to the dirt, sniffing small dust storms. Staring through him. Measuring this apparition in frightening detail.

At the pit's edge, Dash drained the last bit of agave, slid his pickled skeleton into the hole and began to dig again. The mud-caked Rolex on his wrist tolled a silent midnight. There was no more time to waste.

When Dash looked at that Rolex again, it was just past 3 am. Westie's pit had been finished. The pit for Blink was now done. Hok'ee's leather farm gloves stood no chance against the assault waged. Liquid-filled bubbles kept Dash's hands from opening much past a claw.

Crawling for the second canteen, he collapsed. He

managed to get himself over on his back. He gasped and coughed at the water in his throat. He drank to drown himself, but the canteen drained empty. Again, under a blanket of stars, he began to whisper. To sing:

It's dark outside
No moon tonight
Something's comin'
And it don't feel right
Something's comin'
And it don't—feel—

When Dash jerked awake, the horses didn't spook. His boot heels dug deep fissures in the dirt, his knuckles were torn and matted with dried blood. The battle must have been fierce. Startled and confused, he rolled over onto his stomach, hands beside his chest. A marine about to undertake his push-up punishment.

"Oh shit. What time is it?" Focusing the best he could, "Four o'clock. Shit. Four..." Dash popped up off the dirt. His stride deliberate. His determination renewed. He ran down into the arroyo and gathered an armful of wood. He did this many times until the deadwood pile stood as tall as himself. His raging heart invigorated the tequila in his bloodstream as well. A fresh buzz muffled his ears.

Using extra care, he mixed the iron oxide and aluminum powder from the canvas sacks. Four terracotta pots, placed in the dirt, each getting a portion of the mixture. Dash repeated this process until the pots were full. His hands burned with pain as he pressed the four-foot-long visco fuses into each pot.

With the thermite mixed, he lined the bottom of Westie's pit with wood. Snapping larger branches over his knee, he fashioned a makeshift tabernacle, level with the rim of the pit, which would support West's body, and keep it up off the dirt.

The four pots of thermite sat underneath. One pot under West's head. One in between the shoulder blades. The third pot under the small of his back, and the last under his knees, to ensure the most efficient incineration.

With the pots in place, Dash went for Westie. The body was stiff. Spongy. The stench hot, like campfire smoke. An unholy smell. Dash squatted at the head of the ceremonial blanket, skidding his hands under Westie's shoulders.

Hauling up on the body with the little strength that remained, his nostrils filled. He couldn't tamp down the urge to puke. The warm, putrid acid surged from his stomach, drenching the blanket. It kept coming. Waves of heaving as Dash drug the body toward the pit. He couldn't stop now. With West perched face-down on the pit's rim, Dash rolled him over onto his back directly above the pots.

He covered the body with more wood, stood back

and glanced at his wrist. Five-thirty. Dash scanned the horizon and brushed back his matted hair. He snapped the middle buttons of his sweat-soaked shirt and pulled the box of wooden matches from his shirt pocket. Searching the bottom of the saddle bag, he drew out a pack of American Spirits. He inhaled so hard the ash flared and snapped. He calmed himself with the large plume of smoke.

With Blink and Shaman in the arroyo to protect them from the flash, Dash walked to the pit, lit another cigarette and said, "Well, West, it's showtime. No goin' back now, partner." He gathered the four fuses in one hand, and before he could waver, touched them to his cigarette. Dash backed away from the pit and touched himself with the sign of the cross.

When the thermite ignited, Dash was so engrossed and hypnotized, he forgot to not look, just as Hok'ee warned him. The light was gradual at first and then so fantastic, he was forced to turn away. The heat nearly caught the back of him on fire. He ran from the pit like he was being shot at.

The horses' anxious neighs could be heard from the washout. Their snorts and frantic hooves made Dash just as nervous. He cradled his head in his swollen, bloodied hands. His whiskers pricked the raw flesh. He replayed the movie of the last two days. The scene from the morgue. Wishing he got caught on the highway instead of making it to Hok'ee's.

Hell bent on getting through this night, Dash Nelson headed to comfort the horses. He stopped dead in his tracks before disturbing a molecule of desert dirt. A silhouetted figure—his figure—projected up onto Bleeding Rock. The image sent the blood rushing from his head.

sixteen

The massive thermite ignition lasted several minutes. The wood was fully engulfed when Dash was finally able to look at the fire. There was nothing resembling Westie's stiff body left in the pyre. The flames reached ten feet into the night sky. Sparks and smoke rose with the thermals and Dash's thoughts turned to the pony.

The eastern sky began its transition. The horizon shone light grey to delicate blue. Stars began their retreat and a translucent crescent arrived, late to the ball. Dash had gathered up the horses from the washout, and made sure the smoldering campfire was out by taking a long steady piss into the hot embers, his face, black with soot. All except for the crow's feet around his eyes. They were clean. White. Untouched by the night's sins.

Examining his shredded palms, he couldn't quite

determine the blood from the mud. His fingernails stained. Between his hands, his focus shifted to the revolver in his belt. The antique reminder that this was still not over.

Dash was a ghost, drifting slow-motion like a puff of smoke in the desert. Westie's was dying down to reasonable bonfire proportions as he led Blink to the edge of the second, larger pit. Blink didn't resist. Dash was going to have to be certain Blink would fall directly into the pit, as there was no moving a dead nine-hundred-pound horse.

It was at that moment he realized he hadn't made the pit wide enough for Blink to stand broadside. There was no time to dig. No muscle in his body would allow him to attempt such folly. Mountains of dirt surrounding three sides left only one option. He tried to lead Blink between the two pits. The heat and the flames made Blink rear back and throw his head against the lead.

"I'm too tired to fight you on this, goddammit." Dash whispered. "I didn't sign up for this!"

Blink spooked at Dash's elevated voice. Dash raised the revolver, aiming best he could, at the white blaze in the center of the pony's forehead. His hand shook from the weight of the gun. His arm trembled from the heaving in his chest. His fingers cramped up, twitched on the trigger. Didn't even know if he had the strength to pull the thing. But he knew he could not afford to miss.

Dash welled up. His body quaked with sadness.

Collateral damage.

Then, he made a grave mistake. He rubbed his eyes. Mud and soot unleashed their sting. Trying desperately to focus, he did something he never did before.

"Our Father, who art in Heaven, hallowed be thy name..."

Blink cocked his head sideways, enough to stare directly in to Dash's burning eyes. He took a few small steps forward, past Dash's outstretched arm. Past the revolver, and gently pressed his forehead into Dash's chest. Blink grunted—softly. Dash felt the pony's warm breath.

"I can't...this has gotta end." And with that, Dash reared back with all his remaining energy and fired.

seventeen

Up until that moment, Gary Smith, it seemed, had managed to pull off the impossible. He'd kept this story out of the press. The staff at Vanderbilt Medical were tight-lipped, as they didn't need the automatic media circus. Dr. McFadden, fearing reprisal, was making life so miserable for his feckless assistant, that any thought of a media leak by the young lad would most assuredly guarantee him a reservation on one chilly stainless table.

Mr. Smith's Monday morning croissant was absolutely satisfying; right up to the moment his eyes spied the well-dressed figure of Watts standing in his parking space. Instantly, that flaky crust metamorphosed into small meteors and launched through the cosmos of an air-conditioned interior when Gary uttered a resounding, "Shit!"

When Gary walked into his office with Special Agent Watts in tow, Kelly's face showed confusion. She smiled and double checked her calendar. Gary headed her off at the pass, "Kelly, hold my calls." He didn't introduce Watts, nor did he introduce Kelly. He simply opened his office door and directed Watts to enter. Special Agent Watts, recognizing the awkwardness, smiled and nodded at Kelly.

Gary closed the door, removed his sport coat and hung it over the back of his chair, as he always did. Then, he did something he rarely does. He rolled up his sleeves.

"Agent Watts, can I get you some coffee? Water?"

"No thank you. I'm fine."

Watts stood in front of Gary's desk as Gary sat. "Please, sit." Gary's folded hands were the only things on his meticulous desk. "With all due respect, Mr. Watts, I don't have much time. So, if you will, cut to the chase."

"Well Gary, have you seen the news this morning? Seems Mr. Nelson has had a pretty interesting couple-a-days." Watts unbuttoned his jacket and crossed his legs.

Gary was not going to open any doors for Watts. "We've lost a good friend Mr. Watts. It's been a trying time for many of us. I haven't had time to watch the news. If you could dispense with the vagueness, I'd appreciate it."

Watts missed an opportunity. "Please, forgive me. My sympathies for the loss of your friend. I can't imagine how difficult it must be for all of you. I understand you've been together a long time."

Gary nodded, "Yes, we have."

"In the interest of cutting to chase, Mr. Smith, I'd like to ask you about the three-hundred-thousand dollars you transferred into a Bonaccan account a couple days ago."

Gary had put a lot of trust in Dash, given him a long rope and he was trying not to regret it at the moment. "Well, Special Agent Watts, you can ask whatever question you'd like but, that's a private business matter that I don't believe is any business of yours or the FBI's. In fact, I'd like to seriously call into question the basis on which you acquired such information. I believe you might be dangerously closes to treading on my beloved constitution."

Watts adjusted himself in his chair. "The Patriot Act provides many...how do I put this...*unique* avenues for us—the FBI of course, and the Justice Department, when it comes to following large sums of money that might be nefariously acquired."

Watts held up a hand to quell Gary's rebuttal, "If I may continue, sir. Both the U.S Treasury Department and the Justice Department have been investigating secret, anonymous real estate buyers who make large, all-cash purchases with possibly dirty money. Repeated anecdotal information, where we see criminals, with suggested ties to terrorist organizations, laundering money through real estate, suggest to us that this is an area we need to pay attention to."

Gary pressed himself, deep into his chair. "Wow. That's a mouthful, Mr. Watts. I'm impressed. I am. But I'm going to point out some things to you before we end our meeting here. You said, large sums of money that..." Gary formed air-quotes, "...*might* be nefariously acquired? *Possibly* dirty money? *Suggested* ties to terrorist organizations. Sir, do you realize that not one of those words is conclusive?"

Leaning forward, on forearms that could only be attributed to the tossing of alfalfa onto a flatbed, Gary made his eye contact so pointed it was downright uncomfortable.

"Agent Watts, there *might* be purple elephants flying over-head right this very minute. I could, quite *possibly* sue you *and* the FBI for invasion of privacy. I *suggest* you go back to Memphis and reacquaint yourself with the Constitution." Gary stood for the last part. "I believe you know the way out."

Watts wanted to hesitate for a moment longer, but didn't. With a small puff through his nose, wafted, unscathed, trough the double doors. A new approach might be needed. Gary's phone went off in the breast pocket of his blazer at almost the exact time Kelly's voice buzzed in.

"Gary, I have a Mr. Carlton here to see you?"

Gary looked at the text from Jules:

HEADING TO HOK'EE'S RANCH. CALL YOU FROM THE ROAD~ J.

"Kelly, I don't know a Mr. Carlton. Who is he?"

"He's from the Tennessean."

Slowly rolling his French cuffs to their usual position, he wondered how this day might have started if he had ordered the bagel.

eighteen

Shaman alerted a foggy Dash that they'd arrived. Lowering his head to drink, he jerked the reins from Dash's useless fingers. It was all he could do to dismount using his forearms.

A heavy grain sack, drunk with sweet molasses would be the epitome of grace, compared to his haphazard slide to the ground. The arduous task of removing his boots was the first and last he would attempt. The red dirt found its way in. Every fold. Every orifice; and ground away. An earthen exfoliation of a most intimate nature.

Raw, red blisters torn open and stinging with dirt raged when submerged in the cold, crisp water. The cold took his breath. Fully clothed, but not fully undead, he wandered in, almost orgasmic as his ankles submerged. To the knee; his putrid jeans releasing their grasp on the mud. In up to his hips, it resembled a shark attack, the red murk overtaking him like late summer thunderheads overtake the horizon. No longer could he see the small, round river rock under his feet. His sore, swollen balls reveling in the cool turbid waters.

Dash tried to make his hands do more work, scrubbing the dried mud from his hair, his eyes. From everywhere. He felt a very small life return. And, it returned ever so slowly. Not like the one he knew. That was gone forever. The new life. Small—industrious little hummingbird.

He submerged for minutes at a time, listening to the heartbeat that thumped in his ears, the idea of Heaven didn't seem so far away anymore.

nineteen

Dash could see Hok'ee's ranch long before Hok'ee could see Dash. The familiar red barn, the paddock. The house. The ranch was less than a mile away. The sun had tucked itself below the horizon for another night. The purple, starless sky was perfect, unblemished.

From West, with love.

The barn grew larger. He could almost smell the oil leaking from the head valve covers of the old CJ 7, parked by the manure spreader. Dash smiled when he saw the back-door open, the house pouring Hok'ee's color onto the canvas like Moran.

The reservoir had birthed a new resolve. A battle was over, it was time for peace. West deserved it. Dash did, too. He nudged Shaman into a soft canter to close the distance. The old gelding did not protest, eager to get back to sweet alfalfa and dry straw.

Dash quickly noticed something was wrong. Hok'ee was frantically waving his arms, stomping at the earth, gazing up to the heavens. Shouting. Hok'ee's distress caused Dash to look over his shoulder, almost expecting to see the desert floor opening, crumbling in pursuit, to swallow them in a fiery chasm. Nothing of the sort was evident.

When Shaman came to a stop, yards from the house, Dash heard what Hok'ee was saying. "No! What have you done? You've not listened! You've not respected the ways! Dash!" He screamed. "You have dishonored me!" Hok'ee's gesticulations were spooking Shaman. He was grunting and backing down.

Dash's steady hand and gentle nudge from his cowboy heels drove Shaman forward again. "Whoa, now," Dash said, more for Hok'ee than for the horse. "Hoke. I'm sorry..."

"You are sorry? Sorry! Do you understand the ramifications of what you've done? First, you bring a dead man into my home—"

Dash jumped down from Shaman, "Hoke—calm down."

Hok'ee regained his level, "The spirits will punish me for what you've done. I'm old. I've died once. This ranch is all I have. My work. My traditions." He seethed, "You are a brother to me, but you've brought chaos to my home."

"Hoke...I couldn't...I couldn't shoot the pony."

Hok'ee couldn't remain furious with Dash for long. He had been struggling, trying to assuage his guilt for sacrificing the paint in order to honor the spirits. He stood forehead to forehead with Blink, stroking the soft space beneath his big, brown eyes, trying to measure his elation at Blink's return.

Dash stood with Shaman behind him, his chin resting on Dash's shoulder. "Hoke, you're my brother. Chaos in your home is not what I wanted. I know I shouldn't have brought West here. I know that now."

Hok'ee turned and approached Dash, Blink in tow. When he reached Dash, he raised his left hand, in particular his forefinger.

"This ring is to remind me of the chaos that I was as a young man. Your actions were out of love. You honored a brother's request. The spirits—they will judge me and...I will accept my fate."

"Hoke, you're a warrior. You're a survivor. You beat the demons. This ranch. You, your spirit, your honor... it's here—now. That counts. If those spirits think they're gonna fuck with you, they're gonna have come through me to do it. And, Shaman."

Hok'ee recoiled at Dash's hug. "You stink, my friend. Let's get the horses up. There are things I need to tell you, and—things you need to tell me.

A fresh baptism—with soap. After much conversation about the night's events, some dinner and brief, unintended doze off, Dash took up his customary post at the rail for a piss and a smoke. Hok'ee arrived on the porch with tequila and mugs of tea.

"Peyote?" Dash said.

"Peyote? No, you fool. Chamomile."

"Ah—chamomile and tequila—go together like peanut butter and cinder blocks." The two laughed. But, Hok'ee laughed like a man that had things on his mind.

"Dash, Jules called. She's scared. Worried. The FBI is sniffing around Nashville. Everybody is on edge. She's on her way here."

"Ahhh, hell. Here? When?"

"She left this morning. Staying in Gallop tonight. She'll be here tomorrow."

"I won't be here."

"Where you going? What am I to tell her?"

"Look, I'll call her in the morning—from the airport."

"Airport?"

"Yeah, Hoke. The last bit of all this craziness is Bonacca. West wanted me to see Reggie."

"Reggie? Man...you in deep, my friend. Very deep."

"Yeah—the last little bit of all this. Spread his ashes on the North Shore. Then...it's over. I booked it from your office. 9am. Can you drop me off?"

"Of course, we'll take Charlie's truck."

Dash almost spit the mouthful of tequila that danced across his tongue.

"All this time? Still—nobody knows?"

"Nope," Dash said. "You and me friend. Just you an' me."

"Your load is heavy. I thought tonight your mind would rest."

"Not tonight, Hoke. Not tonight."

Part Two

twenty

There was only one person waiting outside the small building that barely passed for a terminal when the De Havilland crept to a stop on the dirt strip, and the spattered, opaque ports couldn't hide her weariness. She adjusted her tousled, walnut locks and brushed her sunken cheeks, applying some invisible sorrow-defying cream. The two shot-glasses of burnt umber found no refuge behind amber aviators.

The Caracole pilot unclipped and gathered his flight logs as the uniformed co-pilot made his way thought the small fuselage to the double aft doors. Dash grabbed his backpack from under the seat. Along with some clothes was a small ceramic vase Hok'ee had given him for Westie's ashes. It would serve as the makeshift urn until he reached the spot where he would set West free.

When the doors opened, the rush of heavy island air mixed with lingering exhaust brought on an immediate skull-crushing headache. He never turned his phone on, nor did he call Jules from the airport, as he said he would.

Impatient and eager to get off the bare-bones commuter before any of the other four passengers, Dash was already crouching at the double-doors when the co-pilot returned with the rickety courtesy stool. Careful not to smack his already throbbing head against the frame, he stepped down and waved a pensive hand to Reggie.

The small island of shrimpers and fisherman was unapologetically Caribbean in its persona. Flip-flops and Bermuda shorts, *pollo* roamed free, evading the *perro callejero*. Dash was noticeably a *turista estadounidense* in his jeans, black t-shirt and cowboy boots. Menstruating anxiety, Reggie met him halfway.

"Hi Dash."

"Reg. How ya doin?" Dash said, mustering an embrace. She was frail. Her arms draped around Dash's neck like broken branches. Her stiff hair scratched his neck when she pulled away. Peppermint tic-tacs and Marlboro camouflaged by too much patchouli. Musty. Humid. Pure sadness. Nothing smells quiet like sadness.

Reggie broke the silence. "Hok'ee emailed."

"Hok'ee? Email? Wow—you still have the same email address."

"You should talk. You've had the same cell number for like fifty years."

"Touché."

Reggie wore a sheer linen bohemian skirt. A satin halter left her tan shoulders bare, and paid just the right amount of attention to her nipples. A silver and leather concho belt rested just below a wisp of navel. The woven wool hobo bag that doubled as her purse seemed to weigh more than she did.

"I'm not sure what I've been dreading more, seeing my dad again, or never seeing him again." Dash's didn't respond. She felt the awkwardness. "I'm sorry. I've been rehearsing this moment my entire life. Now it's here—and—it's nothing like my rehearsals." She tried to retain the detachment she cultivated so carefully. She hated weak, lachrymose girls and grieving widow types. She stomped her dirty foot into the dirt.

Dash tried to help the moment pass. "You got any aspirin in that thing?" Reggie shoved her sunglasses up onto her head and rummaged through her massive, flimsy bag. "Yeah. I should."

She popped the safety top on the generic Ibuprofen, jerking too hard on the bottle, catapulting the tiny, brick-colored tablets entirely into the dirt. "Fuck! Goddamn it!"

Like a trap door in Mother Earth, Reggie was half

visible. Squatting, trying to collect the small tablets, she broke. Her sunglasses, gracefully sliding from her hair, over and past her eyes, catching the end of her nose. Liquid meteors cratered the soft dirt.

"I'm sorry, man," she said, spit lurching from her mouth as she tried to laugh it off. "I'm not a weepy bitch. I'm just…" By now, Dash was squatting across from her. He plucked three Ibuprofen from the dirt and tossed them in his mouth. Reggie didn't look up, she kept at the task at hand, "You need water? You can't take that shit without a drink." She pulled a small, half empty bottle of water from her bag. "Here, take it." It was warm. Dash drank it.

"Reg—" Dash said. "Leave it." He put his hands on her shoulders to help her up.

"I need it." She said, shrugging off his assistance. "This shit's expensive. I—I need it."

Dash squatted again, directly in front of her and lifted her chin so he could see her eyes. "Leave it. C'mon Reg. I'll buy another bottle."

Reggie started crying, "I don't want you to buy me another bottle. I have *this* one."

Dash didn't protest. He stood, took a few steps, wanting only to finish the mission he'd promised Westie he'd finish. He lit a cigarette to calm down, "Okay, Reg."

Reggie stood up, satisfied she'd made her point. She wiped her eyes. Her discount mascara now blended with the airstrip dirt. "I can't play the remorseful daughter, Dash. I don't even know why I'm so upset. I barely knew the son-of-a-bitch."

"Can we not do this here?"

"Do what here? Jesus, Dash! I'm just talking. I'm upset."

"I know you're upset. We're all upset."

Reggie pulled a crumpled, well-used tissue from her bag and blew.

"I need a drink." Dash said. "Let's go see Cholo."

"Sure."

"Does he know?"

Reggie shook her head. "I couldn't tell him."

"Well, let's go tell him. You got a car?"

Reggie laughed. "A car? No, Dash. I have no car. You're gonna have to slum it, babe." She about faced and began walking for the terminal, glancing over her shoulder, nodding for him to close the gap.

Dash flicked his Spirit into the dirt, snuffed it with his boot and mumbled, "It's gonna be a long day."

twenty-one

No matter what the circumstances were, Hok'ee was always glad to see Jules. When her Rover pulled up to the house, he and Turlo met her in the long shadows of the mid-morning sun. The Rover drifted to a soft landing, parallel to Charlie's dusty truck.

The Doisneau-worthy embrace she heaped upon Hok'ee knocked the well-worn Titans cap off her head. Her feet came clean off the ground.

"Hey, Hoke. I'm sorry to barge in on you like this, but I didn't want to talk on the phone. There's too much going on. Too many people in the mix. I hope you don't mind."

"Of course I don't mind. There is a lot to tell you."

Jules Nelson had a gift. She could smile at someone and immediately they'd be struck with the sense that whatever it was that was raining down on them at that very moment would soon be over. She and Hok'ee possessed an understanding of the human condition that went well into that other dimension. Beyond any spoken language, beyond the spaces between the vibrations, and into the minds of hummingbirds.

"Come inside. Let me make you something to eat."

"Oh, I'm not hungry. But coffee would be great." Jules was eyeing the rooms of Hok'ee's place as they made their way to the kitchen. Tradition interwoven with smatterings of the person Hok'ee so desperately tried to survive.

She wanted to ask about Dash. She wanted to lurch into the columns of questions she'd itemized in her mind for the last fourteen hundred and fifty-three miles. Instead, she sat, almost exactly in Dash's musk. Turlo immediately thrust his soiled wet jaws across her crisp white tee, into her chin, furiously tongue-lapping his affections.

The coffee eased her shoulders down to an acceptable level. Her yoga-tuned frame had been twisted by outside forces over the last several days, and the warm swallow in the safe zone of the ranch was welcomed. With the chicory wafting into her nasal passages, she began to feel a center she hadn't felt since the day before Westie died.

"Hoke, this all seems so crazy. I have a lot of questions and I just want the truth." Jules said, with two hands on her mug, leaning forward into the table,

Turlo taking up sentry duties at her boot tips.

Hok'ee nodded, "I know you do."

Jules was searching for the proper way to begin, then she realized there would never be a proper way. "I know he's been and gone. To where, I have no idea. Can you tell me that?"

"Bonacca. This morning."

Jules' eyes widened. "This morning? Goddamn it. With West? Please tell me—"

Hok'ee stopped her mid-sentence. "Jules...I will tell you the whole story. More than you will want to hear. Back to the days in New York City. Has Dash told you about those days?"

Jules nodded, "Yeah, but not much."

"Did he tell you I was messed up on drugs and alcohol? How I was a whore to fame...a false prophet...a liar?"

"He says everyone was messed up during those days."

"I tried to take my own life. Did he tell you that?" Hok'ee blurted it out before he could change his mind. She rocked back in her seat.

"No...he...never told me that. When?"

"Ninety-five."

"Dash and I met in ninety-six but I guess he's never felt it his place to tell me."

"I'm sorry for the lack of subtlety, but I feel that for us to continue, you needed to know that. I've been trying to step from under that shadow for twenty-one years. At some point, we must drag our demons into the light. That point is today. Now, you know."

Jules smiled her smile. "Thank you for trusting me, Hoke. But just so you know, nothing changes. You're who you've always been, a kind and brilliant soul. Family—long before I arrived. I'm blessed to know you. We all are."

Hok'ee warmed their cups. The three of them went to the porch, where pain and sorrow had an unabated path to scatter and dilute on a wide-open expanse able to absorb it, and a wide-open sky, for the hummingbirds.

They took up residence on the large, hand-carved bench with thick cushions, fresh with the dents of Dash's ass. The perfect setting for a long day of remembering.

Hok'ee told Jules almost everything. Reaching far enough back in his memory, to exhume his white man name. Careful that, in reliving the past, he remembered to forget some of the nostalgia that coats his history with a patina, more favorable than that of the metal underneath.

How Terrance struck off with two white men. Joined the circus. Buses. Planes and money. Leaving out, or just barely grazing, stories containing the nubiles desperate to taste them, be tasted by them. He unleashed his condemnation on drugs. The drugs that sipped tequila from young women's navels and fucked them 'til dawn.

"Wow. I knew you all met in Nashville, at the party for Miguel, but I never knew West started his career working for Danny Fields. How'd he go from the New York punk scene to managing Dash?"

"Everyone needs to leave the circus at some point."

"In case you haven't noticed, Hoke, we're still in the circus."

That simple realization dismantled any sense of gravitational order in Hok'ee's cerebral solar system, and he seriously considered drowning that thought in bottle of tequila. But, that would circumvent the affidavit he made with his liver the moment Dash Nelson got out of Charlie's truck at the airport earlier that morning.

"So," Jules said, "since we're being honest, stepping out from beneath shadows and all, you wanna fill me in on this pact? Wanna tell me what Dash is doing in Bonacca? Tell me where Westie's body is."

"You sure you wanna know? Sometimes the horror we imagine ourselves is better than the horror that actually exists."

"Hoke, I've been chasing ghosts across the country for the last three days. I want the truth." A pregnant pause. "Yeah, I'd like some truth."

"Okay."

Hok'ee began searching, again through the attic of

his mind for the facts as he remembered them. Recalled how, after imbibing more than a small wedding party in tequila and Heineken, the three of them, Westie, Dash and himself, wrote into effect the events that transpired a short time prior.

West loved the Native Americans. He donated money and time to bring awareness to the plight of the only people he considered *real* Americans.

Jules was quickly replacing much of the gray on her map with full on color. "So that explains all the benefit concerts for the Navajo Nation schools."

"I don't need to tell you about alcoholism and diabetes on the reservations. West and Dash were our champions. West felt a kinship with my people. From his time as a young boy until this past Friday. I don't try to explain it or understand it. I am simply grateful."

As hard as it was to imagine at the current moment in time, it made sense to them back in the day. Hok'ee told Jules that Dash came to him for guidance and instruction. He told her about the cleansing ritual and he told her about the thermite.

When it came time for Paul James West to pass from this life into the next, he wanted it done the way the Navajo would do it. The way his friend Hok'ee would do it.

The conversation had beaten itself to within inches of its life. Jules had barely touched the lunch or dinner Hok'ee had prepared. Her mind was searching its hard drive, connecting dots and rearranging the colored folders. A new picture had been created and she had to let go of the one she carried. Calm. A shawl, settled around Jules' shoulders, as the events were now clear. At least now she knew.

Jules helped with the plates, glasses and coffee mugs. On the way into the kitchen, she had one more question. "Hoke, I know this was very hard for you. Telling me of your early years, the suicide attempt—I appreciate your trust. I needed to hear those stories. They helped explain a lot of what I never understood about my husband." Hok'ee's silence let her continue. "I don't know what makes him happy. I've been with him for almost twenty years, and I still can't figure it out. He's got the awards, the fame, and he's got money. I couldn't make him happy. I wasn't enough."

Hok'ee saved the water. "Jules, Dash is about the work. He is the work. He had seven brothers and sisters. There was no love left in the house for him. He found it in his work. He loves it. And, it loves him. When he is not creating, he is lost—wandering. It was never you. You—are real love. He'll need that."

With enough to keep her mind churning for days, Jules promised Hok'ee she'd only drive for a few hours and stop if she got tired. The coast clear, Hok'ee realized that little agreement he made with his liver wasn't gonna make it the full twenty-four.

twenty-two

The cab pulled up to Cholo's Beach Bar, Dash in the back, Reggie up front. Dash searched his pockets for money he knew he didn't have. Reggie paid Zim, the driver, one of only three on the entire island, 40LPS for the ride.

"I'll getcha back for the ride once I can get some money," Dash said.

Reggie patted his shoulder as he slammed the door. "And I'm gonna hold you to that. Two bucks, baby. First round's on you," she said. "And, since I'm poor, and you're Daddy Warbucks, all the rounds are on you."

There wasn't an official front door to Cholo's. Off the road, on a small beach, a pier extended sixty feet into the western Caribbean. At the end was a large rectangular boardwalk. In the center, perched on stilts, twelve feet in the air, was Cholo's.

Local fisherman made fast their skiffs to the pier's pilings. Shrimpers were resigned to the north end due to the depths of their vessels. At times, usually in the spring, the random Canadian would stumble upon the pier, ascend the seventeen steps, and immediately have second thoughts about staying for a drink.

No interior decorator was employed to scavenge chandleries for the perfect paraffin lantern to suit the decor. There were no discussions, in sleek Tribeca offices, around glass conference tables regarding the *customer experience*. Cholo's was founded by Cholo.

Beers: 30 LPS
Whiskey and Tequila: 50 LPS
Shrimp, rice and plantains: 141 LPS, cheaper for the locals
Langosta: the same

House specialty, lionfish. Higher classification, Pteroinae. Highly venomous, the uninvited guest was decimating the indigenous species in the reefs. Known to eat almost anything from smaller fish to mollusks, the lionfish has no real natural enemy. Except Cholo.

Locals declared an all-out war, delivering them to Cholo by the hundreds every day. Lionfish Tacos. Zebra Nuggets. Firefish and Caribbean Rice, or, for the North

Americans, should they venture in, Butterfly-Cod and Slaw.

Reggie worked at Cholo's like her mom, Rachel Collins. In 1986, on Westie's thirtieth birthday, a head-on collision occurred when an Annapolis girl who took no shit from nobody meshed metal with Paul West, raconteur. There weren't many photos of her left in the place. Reggie made sure of that.

"Dash! You old son-of-a-bitch! You don't call? Let me know you comin'? Man, you got no love for me. No love." Cholo was ginning ear to ear.

"Hey Chooch." Dash said, patting hard on Cholo's back. "How the hell are ya?"

"I'm good mon, I'm a lover of life." Cholo was Mozambican. His mother fled in 1980 to escape drought and a civil war. A fisherman's existence ended when he 'won' the shack as settlement. "A gentleman's bet," he called it. Neither Dash nor Westie ever questioned it after being directed to the large machete behind the bar, on the wall above the beer fridge. In red marker, along the length of the blade it read, "WANNA BET?"

Cholo chastised Reggie, "This! This is why you not wurkin' today? To run with this charlatan! You betah be careful who you seen wit, girl." Reggie flung her huge purse onto the bar and headed to the fridge for two Heinekens, always kept on hand.

She didn't shoot back in the way she would normally shoot back, or the way her mom used to shoot back. She cocked her head and shrugged her shoulders. Her eyes, teary.

Cholo had seen Reggie cry in drunken stupors more times than he cared to remember. Seen her worry over finances and turn herself blue with frustration over the Rubik's cubes she fancied as suitors. This wasn't that. He turned to Dash, "What's goin' on? You got news you need to tell me?"

"Yeah Chooch, I got news."

Reggie opened the beers, poured three hefty reposado shots, and sat next to Dash. Downing the shot, then chugging most of her beer. She couldn't look at Cholo. Dash lit a Spirit, stalling.

"Chooch, Westie's dead."

Cholo swung his head around slowly, dodging the words, praying they would change. "Ah no. No. No. Can't be." He drank from his beer and walked to one of the large, open cut-out windows. "It just can't be Dash. When?"

Dash filled him in about Westie's untimely death, skipping, of course, the horrid details of the fiasco in the desert. He imagined, for a brief second, the horrified looks on their faces if he recounted tossing West out the morgue window, playing 'turn-me-on-dead-man' with the highway patrolman, or smacking himself in the balls with a shovel—before puking all over West's dead body. The more he thought about it, the more those images triggered a sense of horror in Dash's own complexion.

To catch them up to the current moment in time, he simply said, "West was cremated." Reggie tossed a dubious glance. Cholo was still in disbelief. Dash tried to move along quickly.

"I'm here just for the night, Chooch. I'm heading to the north end, Mangrove Bight, to spread West's ashes. I'd love for you and Reggie to be there. Westie would appreciate it." Reggie let out a blow of air before she could catch it.

"That old piece of land he was gonna build dat house on for him and Ray?" Dash caught Cholo sternly. Reggie saw the exchange.

"What old piece of land? What Ray—my mom? Dash...Chooch! You guys know where my mom is? You've been speaking to her?" She was ramping up quickly.

"Whoa, Reg!" Dash said, "Nobody's been talkin' to your mom. Chooch?"

Cholo shook his head wildly. "No way, Reg. I'm sorry. I'm talkin' about a long time ago. Before you were born. I'm all messed up with this right now. I would never betray you...your trust. I have not spoke to dat woman since dat day. The same day you last saw her." Reggie poured more tequila, smoked another cigarette, and drifted back down to earth. A feather from a startled pigeon, beholden by gravity.

At that moment, Cholo remembered something very important that needed mentioning. "Dash. You got another problem. Man, it's gonna be a bad day here real soon."

"I'm leaving tomorrow. I'm gonna stay at Reggie's tonight. I thought we'd all get out there first light, do a small send off. Then I'd be on my way."

Cholo and Reggie exchanged glances, "Well, the island's about to riot." Reggie said, nonchalantly. "Been talkin' about it for weeks, but now, the referendum came down yesterday and folks are pissed."

Dash was confused. Cholo chimed in, "The big boys— gas and oil men—they paid somebody some big money on the mainland. Trying to develop the island here. Gonna levy a major gas tax on us. You know, man...everything needs to be brought in from the mainland. Dey know none of us can pay what dey will ask for gas—for our boats. Food for our families. Clothes. Dey gonna starve us out. People here gonna explode. You in trouble here, man. You gotta go. Now!"

"Look Chooch, Reg, I gotta finish this thing." Dash reached into his backpack and pulled out the small urn with Westie's ashes. Cholo was on his way to the fridge for more alcohol, and he was directly abeam of the urn when it landed on the wood bar with a well-packed thud.

Reggie's voice changed pitch, down three half-steps.

"Holy shit! That's him?"

"That's him."

Cholo stuttered, "No way man. Westie was a big boy. That ain't all-a-him."

Dash readjusted his Ray-Bans up on his forehead, "Well, no—it ain't *all* of him. I couldn't bring *all* of him. I'm lucky I got this much."

Reggie, with a dubious look, said, "Whaddaya mean, 'you were lucky enough to get this much?' Dash...are you fuckin' with us? If you're fuckin' around, you are one sick bitch."

"I'm not fuckin' around, Reg! Chooch, this is Westie. I know it's small, but it's Westie. Both of you...can you just...sit down." Dash searched, and thinking it would clarify things, he blurted, "Reg, your dad wanted to be a Navajo."

"What? I thought West was from New Jersey,"

"Yes, Chooch—please let me finish before you...either of you ask any questions."

Reggie said with closed eyes, "Can you pass me that bottle? Chooch, I'm gonna need another beer, too."

"Are you done?" Dash said.

Reg smiled and nodded. "Mm, hm."

When Dash finished telling Reggie and Cholo about the events of the last few days, he found it all hard to believe himself. Having to leave out some of the major details created untraversable gaps. The inebriation didn't help. The night was careening headlong into the dawn. Everyone needed to go home, there was simply too much of the elephant left to chew.

twenty-three

The seventeen steps up to Cholo's were murderous after a night of heavy drinking. The last of the apocalyptic zombies stammered down the dock. Cholo, always with a keen ear for a distant splash, ready with a fisherman's pole. Dash, Reggie and Cholo still sat at a table by the stairs, the last of the reposado saturating the cigarette butts. One finger of rum teased the brave soul who dared to venture to that depth.

Bleary eyed and unsteady, Dash patted Reggie on the back, "Let's go, kid." She burped, a cavernous sound more akin to a lumberjack than a petite island granola girl, and laughed out loud.

Dash's nostrils filled suddenly with the low, fetid, odor; mephitic and abdominal. He gagged, "Lovely. At's just lovely."

Cholo wiped at the air, "Oh lord, woman!"

"Well you know what they say," Reggie said, thrusting her arm up into the air, extendus maximus; Her middle finger, the phallus, finger-banging her lewdness unapologetically, "part of being a woman is...knowing when...not to act like a lady. Or some shit like that."

Dash put Westie in the backpack and lifted Reggie up from her armpits. "Okay woman, not a lady, let's go home before you turn into Jack the Ripper."

"Who?" Reggie started laughing a drunk's laugh, snorting, singing as she slowly John Wayne'd her way down the stairs.

"Happiness is a warm gun,
Chu-go-ba-dehr,
Chu-go ba-dher, ba-deher, wount wow"

Cholo walked to the top step with Dash. "I don't remember that part of the song, man."

Dash laughed as she completed the descent, sat on the pier, cross-legged, and lit a cigarette, "Yeah, I think that was Lennon's demo version." Both got a chuckle.

Cholo turned serious. "Dash man, this riot shit is for real. I'll meet you and Reggie, then you gotta get outta here. No joke." Cholo's voice was calm, deep and sincere.

"Okay, Chooch. Pick us up at five-thirty so we can catch the sunrise. Once we've set West off, I'll head straight to the airstrip. There's only one flight tomorrow. I'm on it. It's all good."

They shook hands and Cholo pulled Dash in for another embrace. "It's good to see you. I wish under better circumstances. But it's good to see you."

Dash turned and carefully descended the stairs. From the bottom, he shouted up, "See you in a couple hours!" Cholo glanced at his watch and winced. Yesterday had run headlong into today.

Reggie was gelatin. Drunk gelatin. The only way she was making it to the road was on Dash's back. From the shadows of the tree-lined road, Cholo heard his employee. "Go back! Dash—I lost my fuckin' flip flop!"

twenty-four

When Zim pulled up to Reggie's place, she and Dash were out cold in the backseat. Most of the island was asleep. Stray dog, iguana and whore found a mound of trash to lay on. Zim wanted a mound to lay on, too. Getting this fetid duo out of the car was his last assignment.

Lovers wasn't the word Zim would use to describe what he and Reggie were at one time. But, whatever word it was that one would use, Reggie had many. And it usually ended with her being dropped off.

"Okay, you two! Wake up! It's late...you need to get out of my car!" Zim pounded the metal roof, shaking Dash awake.

"Holy shit, man!" Dash shook Reggie. She was not moving. "Reg! Let's go. We're home," he said, gently slapping her flushed cheeks.

Zim was impatient. "Jesus man, what'd you two get into up der? I seen her in bad shape, but dis is some shit."

"She's had a bad day." Dash's exit was that of an unrehearsed clown posse leaping from an armored truck heist. Leaning hard into his door, he wiped a clean swath on Zim's cab, from the rear quarter panel, around the trunk to Reggie's door. Jerking the handle, she fell out into his sloppy grasp and woke up.

"Shit—I feel like shit," She slurred.

"I'm not waiting for you to search that bag." Zim shouted. "I'll be an old sack by dah time you get my money. I'll find you."

Zim began to pull away, then stopped and reversed in a quick spurt. "Hey man," he said to Dash, "Things gonna get serious real fast. You and Reggie in a bad spot right here. She better be upright real quick."

Dash missed the intel. "I'll get you yer LPs, man. No worries. I'll find you tomorrow." Zim, exasperated, spun the rear wheels.

Dash struggled with Reggie's dead weight against his own suspect form. Luckily there were no witnesses as the two rolled-up wet carpets pin balled their way to the door.

The foliage-enveloped house, just barely taller than a commercial dumpster, sat as the termination of a dissuading swath of sand through the low brush. The chalky yellow clapboard clung perilously to the shack's framing. Slightly skewed windows and doors gave it a funhouse appearance. The only thing truly discernible as something once was the mailbox, full of weeds. An Ubangi, caved in at the skull by a dislodged coconut.

Inside, Dash sat Reggie on a couch whose best days were during the Nixon administration. A "living" room, Reggie's room, and a small five-by-six out crop disguised as a bathroom with constantly dripping faucets comprised the hut.

Well-worn panties—animal print, hopeful satin, and grey lace, once white with innocence—found their way onto the kitchen table, bathroom and sink. Her 32Bs rested snugly in the lacy slings of Victoria's Secret and Maidenform, which, when given the night off, rested on the backs of chairs and the floor. There were clean clothes, dirty clothes and clothes hovering in a state somewhere in between. Strewn about were books, magazines and cigarettes. Lots of cigarettes.

And every inch of the place reeked of Reggie; a princess who missed the bus uptown and stands caught in the rain on Prince Street and Mott, longing for the shelter of Lombardi's Pizza's awning, her heel jammed firmly in a storm drain. So fucking close.

Shoving aside a pile of panties, bras, jeans and a towel, Dash tried to close the door to piss. Too many shampoos, soaps and creams crowded the space. Two blow-dryers hung on the lone towel rack—one had the plug jerked clean off. A tiny wire basket lay smothered under an avalanche of cotton balls, toilet tissue and cleansing wipes.

He ran his hands under the steady trickle from the faucet and wiped them on something resembling a towel. When he exited, Reggie was no longer on the couch.

"I'm fuckin' starving," She said, head buried in the Philco V-handle. "You hungry, Dash? I'm fuckin' hungry."

"No," Dash blinked. "I'm not. Can't even think about food right now." Dash plopped his frame onto Reggie's sofa, immediately regretting it. A fugitive spring jabbed the back of his knee just below the thigh. That bit of unhappiness was overtaken a millisecond later when his coccyx bone met a wooded cross-brace in the sofa's frame, just below the cracker thin cushion. He was now wide awake. "Jesus Christ!"

Reggie turned around, munching a piece of Kraft cheddar cheese. "Oh shit, don't sit on that side," she mumbled, "it's fucked."

Dash scoffed, "Really? Thanks for telling me, Reg." Reggie closed the door with her foot and sat across from Dash in an oversized chair. She reeled in her drugstore feet, tucked them up under her skirted knees, and picked at the square of cheese.

"There's so much I gotta tell ya. I don't even know where to start. It's too late—I'm too damn drunk." Dash scooted his throbbing spine over to the left in an attempt to meet the amiable part of the sofa. He leaned his swimming head back on the crown, letting his Ray-Bans slowly drift from his forehead to some figment of clothing below. He lifted his suede Ranch Hands, one heel crossing over the other onto Reggie's unsteady coffee table.

He could hear the window unit humming in her bedroom. The ceiling fan above clipped out a tempo, the eighth notes measured by the small chain clicking against the bulbous glass that no longer shared its glow. The sweet lyric to *Too Many Bridges* began in his head.

Too many bridges between here and home
And it's such a drag to have to do it alone
I got so much to tell you but I don't know how
Across the great divide between then and now

The incredible explosion might have passed for a kick drum drenched in reverb if the entire house didn't shake.

"It's happening!" Reggie yelled as she jumped up, seemingly sober after a week-long sleep. First, to the table where her massive, woven bag lay, and then to her bedroom. Dash frantically looked for something to gather as well, but his bag was packed, laying exactly where he dropped it when he came in.

"What the hell was that?" Dash said.

"The riot! They started the riot!" Reggie galloped through her house, drifting around the furniture, almost in slow motion. All at once, she was on Dash. "Let's go! We gotta go." The fog hadn't quite let Dash go from its grasp. He drifted behind Reggie like a small dinghy with not enough keel. Yawling, fighting to get his legs—that seemed to occur just after the second explosion.

Reggie was spry and fleet-footed, like a small squirrel. "We gotta find Zim. He can take us to Kim's, on the south rim. The riot won't reach down there."

Dash was dazed, tired; hopelessly shit-faced. Running through the sand streets in suede cowboy boots was like running on a frozen lake. "The south rim! We gotta meet Chooch."

Reggie cut him short. "We're not meeting Chooch, Dash. There isn't going to be an ash ceremony. This entire island is going up in flames!"

There were a dozen cars on the island, only three of them for hire, and they needed one. Reggie drug Dash through the streets looking for Zim. When she spotted his car coming straight at them, she pulled up short, waving. "Zim! Zim! Hey!"

The cab skidded to a stop, he didn't let her talk, "Reg, I told you! I told you it was coming!"

Reggie had her hands on the door jam. "Z...you gotta take us to Kim's!"

Zim recoiled. "Kim's! Girl you mad! I'm not driving

you down der! They blowing up anything that's moving. I'm goin' to the pier—you should be goin' der, too! The only place they not gonna burn is Chooch's place." Zim gunned the engine, the car disappeared into the darkness.

"Reg—forget the south rim! Let's get to Chooch's place. He's right, they ain't gonna burn Cholo's." Reggie sank. They— she...just let their one and only ride disappear into the darkness.

twenty-five

With Zim's car long gone, Reggie grabbed Dash by the hand and the two headed toward the small town center. Father Dominic pleaded for cooler heads, right up until the gunfire erupted, scattering everyone, including the good father.

Dash and Reggie flung themselves into the dirt, unsure if it was for effect or for real. Dash took over. "Listen, we're not gonna make it on foot. We gotta find another way." On their hands and knees, it was hard to scan the horizon from whence the shots were fired.

Breathing heavily, Reggie said, "I'm open to ideas. You can call in the choppers anytime, superstar."

Dash grabbed her by the arm and lifted her hard. "Let's go." Just past the cathedral, the main road bent off to the perimeter road, the one to Cholo's.

In 1998, Hurricane Mitch cut the island clean in half. The first bridge erected over the 'cut' was rickety and didn't last but one season. The new bridge, the concrete one that was still standing, was paid for by anonymous donations from a well-to-do music man. Dash was hoping it would still be standing when he and Reggie needed to cross.

At the junction of the main road and the perimeter road stood Raeff's Outpost. Operating as a post office and general store, Raeff's collected old men and their dominoes like an eddy collected sand. On this riotous evening, a small pink scooter leaned unaccompanied against the crumbling stucco wall. Dash grabbed Reggie. "Your ride's here."

With a small cough, the 50cc motor whizzed to life. With Reggie on the back, wearing Dash's backpack, her purse mashed between them, Dash barely fit on what remained of the pointed seat. Reggie's feet were on the pegs, Dash's thrust straight out on either side, putting the exclamation point directly on his tender tailbone. The glorified weed-eater crawled painfully to its top end.

"C'mon! You piece of shit!" Clambering away from the town square, the engine bogged quickly midway up the small rise, the last obstacle before a curvy descent to the bridge. Dash's wrist ached from torquing the throttle. What should've been deep, dense fauna, was glowing amber. Shadows darted in the lane. Dash didn't let up.

Reggie was yelling over the squealing two-stroke. "That's the bridge!"

Gaining momentum from the slope of the hill, the needle on the speedometer was quivering around the 40-mph mark. Dash glanced down for just a second. The sharp bend to the bridge shouldn't have surprised him. His eyes widened.

Most of the bridge was gone into the washout below. Only a small tentacle of concrete kept the north side from drifting off into the Caribbean. Chunks of concrete, some large, some brick-sized, littered the roadway. Splinters, remains of wooden safety rails scattered like matchsticks. Dash squeezed hard on the front brake, locking the ten-inch wheel. The soft sand swallowed the small wheel, jerking it hard. Dash's grip on the handlebar was firm. His left hand shot away from his body, taking him with it. His right elbow careened into his rib cage. The scooter dive-bombed into the dirt.

Dash and Reggie resembled a synchronized swimming routine. Slow motion tumbling, limbs flying in unison, a cloud of fine dust shown in the single candlelight luminescence of the wanting headlight. Each of them skidded to a stop before reaching the jagged, blown open chasm.

Dash's backpack however, did not stop. The last thing either of them saw was the urn, tumbling, dispensing a little more of Westie with each bounce before breaking in two and disappearing over the edge, followed shortly by Dash's backpack.

Dash managed to roll onto his stomach for the final vision. "You have got to be KIDDING me!"

Reggie was in pain. Her light skirt and halter gave no protection from the dirt and rocks. She was skinned, cut and bleeding. "Oh my god Dash...I'm so sorry. I couldn't hold it!" She was crying.

Both crawled towards the edge and peered into the swift current of the cut below. "Well—I'm just gonna take a chance here and say, that was probably NOT the way West wanted to go." Reggie was hurt. The attempt at levity, a disaster. "Can this day get any fuckin' worse?" Dash looked at Reggie, who had no answer. "Can it?"

Once on their feet, they assessed their situation, Reggie stepped towards the remaining small ledge of the bridge. "There's enough...Let's try!"

Dash caught her by a scraped arm. "No. It's not strong enough. If it collapses, we're in the water. That'd be a bad thing, Reg." Surveying, Dash said, "Whatcha got now, kid? Cause we ain't making it to Cholo's tonight."

twenty-six

"Let's go back," Reggie said. "We can head down Loop Road, by the marina. Maybe it's safe down there." The gunfire was frequent. Dash wondered what scores were being settled in the shadows cast by those not willing to be slaves again.

A light-gauge rusty chain securing the gate presented little protest to Dash's heel. The Marina Municipal was home to three commercial fishing boats, six open skiffs, and a handful of blow boats, sailed there by dreamers and then left there by the pragmatist they'd become after a few nights of sound sleep on solid ground.

"We can hang here. Hopefully they just blow right by."

Halfway down a shaky finger pier, Dash's eye landed on the lichen-covered hatch of a twenty-seven foot

Vega. It was a less than stellar option, but it was the only unlocked vessel on the pier.

"Get on," said Dash.

"This! This is the boat you pick?" Dash shushed her. "Dash," she said whispering loudly, "This goddamn boat is barely floating. Can't we pick another one?"

"Reggie...they're all locked. Get on. Now!"

A spelunker with a most colossal spirit for adventure might twist a gut at the truly dark, musty air in the shut up cabin. The floor boards were drowning, clunking; drifting as far as they could go in such a small space. Leaking ports, leaking hatches; leaking. The cushions, sopping wet, hazardous with the same black spots of mold that streaked the entire cabin.

A pair of bloated brook frogs bobbed gently against the cabin sides, rocking from the motion of Dash and Reggie's shifting weight, belly-up, tiny blobs of limbed dough in an algae-choked deep-fryer. Halyards and hardware clanked against the mast. Cans and bottles stowed below rattled to life with the shifting weight. Dash tried to settle Reggie who looked like she was about to blast off. "Listen, it's not ideal. But we need to sit tight until the sun comes up."

The evening buzz-kill was upon Reggie. The pain from her cuts, front and center. The stagnant water, the mold, dead frogs; ambushed. A real-life waterspout of dankness. Reggie didn't have time to cover her mouth. She spewed into the small galley sink. The putrid potpourri caused spasms in Dash's abdomen as well. He reached for the companionway ladder.

Blood rushed to his face. The whirling dervishes of Rage, Hope and Despair made for a crowded vessel. "Reg—my phone. My phone was in the backpack. My passport, wallet, everything. We've got nothing. We can't call anyone." He played it again, to make sure. "I can't call anyone." Dash ran his hands through his hair. The cuts and bruises began to settle in. He was feeling a surge. His temples throbbed. That Brahma charging.

twenty-seven

With his elbows resting on either side of the companionway hatch, Dash could hear the approaching maelstrom. Pupils dilated, ears pitched like a fox, the riot was coming. Dash dipped below to find Reggie rinsing the putrid sink with a different putrid water from the bilge. He thought about making a bad joke. He didn't. Instead, he sloshed through the cabin, searching for anything that might be useful.

In the small nav desk, he found a black aluminum mag light. His excitement plummeted when it failed to illuminate. Corroded.

On the forward bulkhead hung a small, brass Weems and Plath paraffin lantern. Skeptical that they weren't filled with the same green water, Dash removed the small glass chimney and pinched the wick. "Reg—you got a lighter in that bag?" Reggie scoured her duffle purse for the pink Bic. Dash flicked it once, "Here goes nothin'," he said.

The small flame licked at the soaked cotton. A tiny blue flame caught its breath and glowed yellow. The heat and black smoke made Dash cough. "I'll be a mother..." Dash smiled at Reggie. "You believe that?"

Reggie stood by the sink, unsure if her quaking dry heaves were finished. "Lucky us," she spat, "Now we can actually see how bad it is down here."

Dash went to Reggie. "Reg—I need ya. I need you to keep it together right now. We gotta get some rest. These windows are gonna be glowing like all get-out. It's gonna be hard to hide."

Reggie was exhausted and hurt. "What do you want me to do?"

"Help me find something to cover these port lights with."

Dash began searching the small cabin. Reggie was searching, too. Searching in the sense that her eyes were, in fact, projecting a retinal image, but she wasn't really seeing a damn thing.

She dug a small first-aid kit from a cubby in the head compartment. Under the galley sink, a bottle of bleach and some hard, curled sponges. A small electrical panel hid itself under the companionway ladder. Dash stopped in his tracks. *What are the odds*, he thought to himself.

A quick flick of the small red lever yielded nothing.

In the bluish glow of the moon, Dash pined for the soft light of his studio and a glass of the good stuff; the cursor in his brain roaming from E Flat Major to Electrical Prognostication.

What seemed to be an hour, lasted a second. His eyes fixated upon the shore power connection in the cockpit. He scraped at the contacts with his finger nail and jammed the cable back in. Down below once again, he flicked the small switch a few more times, cursing the hapless vessel. With the timbre of a honey bee, the small bilge pump hummed to life and began to suck the water down. Dash turned to Reggie with raised eyebrows and his long-forgotten smile. "Things are looking up," he said.

Reggie smiled sarcastically, flashing two thumbs up. "Awesome."

Floor boards in place, Dash wrestled a permanently creased Dacron sail from a yellow sail bag in the v-berth and draped it along the port side settee. "Reg—sit down. Get some rest. I'm gonna douse this lantern. It sounds like things are heating up out there." Reggie curled up, fetal position. Dash tucked the reminder of the sail around her bruised body. Her bare shoulder, crusted with brick colored blood, shown in the shaft of a muted blue. "We're gonna have to get these cuts cleaned out," he said. She grinned a tight-lipped smile. She was drifting off. He let her sleep.

It was the flickering glow in his eyelids that woke him. The sky itself was a lighter hue. If everything had gone as planned, they'd be with Chooch right about now.

Not sure how long he'd been out, he missed the explosion. A fishing boat a few hundred feet to starboard was ablaze. They were at the fence. Dash crouched in the companionway and, under cover of the yellowed dodger, managed to glimpse a dark figure. A sudden spark of light illuminated a body reared back, arm extended in perfect form. The figure heaved a Molotov cocktail over the fence.

The jar of petrol made a glorious high arc before crashing on deck of a steel research vessel. A small tsunami of liquid flame engulfed the foredeck and windshield. Dash's eyes shown white. "That's too close." He whispered to himself. "Too close." He spied Reggie, still sound asleep on the settee. He knew it was only a matter of moments before the criminal mob would discover the kicked-in gate. Euphoric destruction had no rationale.

Dash began whispering to himself again. "Think man. Think." He surveyed the flotsam of which he was now part of. "Oh, you little ship...can you pull this off? Can you?" Crawling through the cockpit, he unplugged the crusty shore power cable and gently laid it on the dock. Trying not to rock the narrow boat, he stepped lightly to the mast, uncoiled the stiff, algae-stained halyards and removed the sun-baked mainsail cover, the fabric disintegrating into small flecks as he pulled.

The two fishing boat interiors were fully ablaze. Adjacent wooden dock pilings caught fire without protest. The creosote inferno sent smoke and flames high into the night sky. The marina was lit up as if amber search lights blasted down from rescue choppers. The heat was reaching the small Vega where Reggie slept unaware and Dash, now huddled in the cockpit, delayed the inevitable.

When the rioters found the kicked in gate, Dash knew it would be mere minutes before they were discovered. Adrenaline pumped at a rate fast enough to douse the pain from the crash. He hopped directly from the cockpit to the dock and set about unhitching the boat.

The three-strand line might just as well have been steel cable, welded in a permanent figure eight lashing around their dock cleats. Cursing to himself, he lumbered about the small finger pier. "Goddamn it!" Keeping an eye on the advancing gang of thugs, he tossed off the last of the cruddy bow lines, and shoved with all his might. He waited too long.

Jumping aboard mid ship, Dash darted again to the mast. The boat listed to port. It's bow swung slowly toward the harbor channel and again he questioned everything. The eternal observer, knowing that as one thing is observed, it is changed by the observation itself, must look carefully at the deep shit in which he finds himself, should he find himself in deep shit. The universal truth that bore a hole through his cerebral cortex at the present moment was that a man can change his mind right up to the point where he can't no more.

It's showtime, West. Flip the switch, he thought, tossing the remains of the Sunbrella sailcover into the cockpit. With the mainsail uncovered, he began to haul down hard on the line. Praying, with each over-hand tug, that it would not snap. The creased, decrepit mainsail rose from the boom like a ghost. They weren't invisible anymore.

twenty-eight

The commotion on deck stirred Reggie. Something felt different. She opened her eyes and tried to focus. Her mind was slow to discern the pounding and thumping from above as footsteps. Dash's heavy bare footsteps.

Reggie made her way to the companionway, still shrouded in a light fog. She poked her head up just far enough to see Dash at the mast securing the main halyard. She turned to where the dock once was. Her fog lifted immediately.

"Dash! What are you doing?"

"Get back inside, Reg."

The rioters had abandoned individual conquests within the boatyard, and honed their focus on a single target, the escaping boat. A few reached the end of the pier faster than Dash thought possible. By his estimation, the boat had forty yards on the dock, surely none of them were about to swim. Dash felt a bit of relief at that thought. It was short-lived.

He could plainly see one of the delinquents manifest the glowing glass jar. Another produced the spark. The dangling rag burst into flames. Reggie had not gone inside.

"Dash! He's lighting something!"

"I see that, Reg."

Forty yards was nowhere near enough distance. As he reared back to toss the flaming cocktail, Dash noticed the boat was lumbering, broadside to the dock.

"We gotta turn the boat...give a smaller target."

He dove for the cockpit. His jeans wet and heavy below the knee, sagged and bunched around his ankles. The bottom of his 501s snagged a deck cleat at that critical moment of take-off, causing him to stumble and crash down hard on the brittle tiller, snapping it off just forward of the rudder post.

He landed hard. The dull thud of his head hitting the cockpit coaming resulted in a clean, razor-sharp gash at his hair line.

"Holly shit!" Reggie screamed. "Are you okay?" She had taken her eyes off the third-world pitcher. She didn't see his toss to the plate. Dash shook the stars from his head. A warm trickle drew a crooked line between his brows to the tip of his nose, and dotted the gelcoat. He untwisted himself in time to see the glowing mason jar slam into the stern and explode.

A riotous cheer arose from the dock. The water burned. Black smoke and heat stung Dash's and Reggie's eyes. The boat maintained her motion away from the dock but the fatal blow had been dealt. Distance was not the issue now.

Dash raised up and began to wage war on the flames with the tattered sail cover, slamming at the stern wildly. Clouds of chalky dust mixed with the black smoke. Calcified bird shit and gasoline. With each desperate slash, the sail cover broke the water's surface and made way on the flames. The fiberglass puckered, the gelcoat black with soot. Dash's eyes now stung with salt water. Blood spattered with each swat.

A drowning swimmer.

A shark attack.

He felt good about their chances. Then Reggie spoke. "Dash—he's throwing another one!"

Dash didn't want to look. Didn't want to stop his street fight but he couldn't help it. He glanced up momentarily. Long enough to see the incendiary device floating in the night sky. Exxon's comet, towing its black con-trail. Everything seemed to freeze. Time. Wind. Sound.

It all went dead.

What Dash heard next took him back to his days as a kid. When he would find the biggest rocks he could, and toss them from the railroad trestle. The splash always made two distinct sounds. The sound of the stone hitting the water, followed by the sound of the water itself.

KA-BLOOP!

That's the sound that snapped him back.

Reggie blasted off. "Fuck you! You...fuckin' ASSHOLE! You missed! FUCK YOU!" The fire was smoldering at best. He kept at it, dipping the burned remnants of the sail cover into the water and swiping the stern until it smoldered no more.

"I think we're far enough..." Dash said, winded. "We don't have to worry about him reaching us with another one." The pain arrived in his ribs. Tiny rivulets of blood thinned by salt water filled the creases in Dash's face. Reggie sat beside him. The boat heeled with the small puff of breeze. Behind them, the rioters dispersed.

Amid the chaos, the burning boats and fading voices, Reggie pinched the gash in Dash's head. They could hear the distinct sound of an outboard pull cord. Arguing, yelling; hoodlums turning on each other.

Reggie said, "What if they get that thing started?"

Dash looked over his shoulder towards the dock and then glanced up at the mainsail, "Well, it won't hold all of em. If they had guns, they'd-a shot us by now. So—that's the good news."

Reggie scoffed, "Ha! The good news? 'If they had guns they'd-a shot us.'" She burst out laughing. Dash laughed with her. The outboard roared to life. They stopped laughing.

"What are the chances this furler works?"

"What's a furler?"

Dash untangled the furling line on the port side and released the slimy jib sheets. To all things beautiful and dutifully built, time is the enemy. Sun, salt and neglect wreak havoc. Maybe there was just enough life in the old girl to last the night.

The jib rolled out half-way and jammed solid. The boat tilted slightly. Steering with the nub of a tiller was difficult and with each knot of speed, became increasingly worse. Dash needed Reggie distracted while he pondered what might actually happen should that boatful of scoundrels reach them.

"Reg—I need you to look around. Find something we can lash to this tiller. We need to make it longer."

She looked confused, but willing. "Okay..."

The skiff's bow, spreading a wide wedge, clawed toward them. "Oh, my god," Reggie said. Dash tried his best to focus on getting the sailboat to move faster.

"How many? Can you see how many?"

Reggie raised her forefinger, poking the air as if she were popping tiny bubbles. "Five. There's five of 'em. Four up front, one driving." Dash's mind raced.

"We ain't gonna out-run 'em."

"So... what do we do?"

"We could ram 'em," he said. Reggie looked terrified

at the thought. "I mean, we don't have enough speed but we could take a chance and try to run the fuckers over."

"You think that would work?" Reggie's fingernails clung to a ledge of hope about as thick as a quarter.

"No."

"No! Why say it then!"

"I'm—thinking...out loud."

"They're getting close!"

And just like that, as quickly as it roared to life, the outboard shut down. The bow of the small skiff dipped. The yelling began again, each of them taking turns pulling the start cord, as if the other could possibly be doing it wrong. Dull sputter after dull sputter, the small skiff sat at the mercy of the channel current. It turned beam to the wind, and slowly, methodically, drifted back towards the burning pier.

"I'll be damned," Dash said, "You gotta turn the fuel cock on, boys. Shoulda learned that in Riots 101." Dash could have sworn the damn skiff winked at him.

There was no laughing, simply disbelief. Reggie looked at Dash, slightly, ever-so-delicately shaking her head.

"Can I ask you something?"

"Sure."

"Do you have any idea whatchur doing?"

"Kinda."

"Can I ask you something else?" she said, in an eerily

calm voice.

"Yep."

"Where we goin'?"

Without missing a beat, Dash replied, "I thought we'd grab a hot shower, head to The Palm for dinner— maybe check out a movie or something."

Reggie erupted in laughter. Dash followed shortly, the two howling in the dark. Dash grabbed his ribs, remembering the crash onto the tiller. He coughed a gurgling, liquid cough into his hand. Reggie saw the blood before he did.

twenty-nine

The sun was fully up. Dash sat shirtless in the cockpit, drawing on a cigarette he found in Reggie's purse. Fighting the weariness, hunger and dehydration, he coerced himself to his feet. He needed to get below and check on Reggie. Standing over her, he thought about her life. He thought about how he knew nothing much beyond her false carapace and guarded outbursts.

He scanned her bruised, scraped body. The wounds black with dirt. The pain in his ribs kept his breathing shallow and murky. His mind went briefly back to her mom Rachel. To the days when she and West were hot and heavy. Making love all afternoon, then meeting up with Dash and Hok'ee at Cholo's for a night of raucous storytelling. Exaggerations, at one time—not anymore. Excess. Reckless abandonment. And now—a few feet away lay the casualty.

Sound asleep on the dirty sail, her hippie skirt in tatters, skinned knees tucked up in the fetal position. Filthy feet, at a weird angle, looked amputated from the ankles. Dash tapped gently on the only undamaged part of her shoulder, never expecting her to shake awake so violently.

"Whoa...whoa...it's okay. Everything's okay," She scanned the boat. The sunlight creased her eyes. "We gotta dress these cuts. They get infected out here, we got major problems."

"Oh—" Reggie grunted. "I thought we already had major problems."

"Wait 'til I start cleaning these things."

She sat upright. Dash put a hand on her shoulder.

"Can you stand up?" Reggie rose, one hand on the bulkhead to steady herself.

"Who's driving the boat?"

"The boat's driving the boat. It's barely moving. We got some time." Dash squatted down in front of her. The adrenaline drip had been pinched off. In the moments between bullets, those in foxholes regain their vision. They get to count the dead, feel for holes. Pain creeps through a sluice of calm.

"Turn around."

Reggie turned, revealing to Dash her left side. He tried, unsuccessfully, to diminish the reaction. "Wow... Okay, girl. We're gonna get a little up close and personal here. Uh—I'm sorry... but this thing's gotta come off."

She thrust her thumbs into the waist band of the flowery skirt and shoved it to the floor. Skylab might have been the only thing that fell faster than Reggie's skirt when it came to a man squatting in the general proximity of her vestibule. The sun rises. The earth turns. Reggie drops her skirt.

For her, the moment lacked any hint of awkwardness or reservation. In Dash, a great discomfort welled. Tea kettles whistled. Pistons pumped the wrong chemicals into the wrong shafts. Soiled wounds did little to disguise a perfectly proportioned stern in Tiffany-blue panties. His face was inches from her crotch. Eyeing her gentle mound, under a veil of thin satin, caused an unsanctioned rise in his heart rate. A small mutiny was also rising.

In the midst of a deep despair, when the self's reflection projects only a building crumbling in the great conflagration, the winds of the soul blow wretched, and the good book fails, a man need only brush his lips across the soft mons of a woman. Her spirit of hartshorn will most assuredly arouse a new consciousness and restore order to the Republic.

This was not a vicinity, Reggie's vicinity—in which Dash needed to dwell. Nor could he entertain any further investigation of what might be behind the veil flanked by the nubile thighs. This night, and quite unexpectedly, Reggie became a woman.

Also quite unexpectedly, Reggie untied her strafed halter and lifted it over her head. In her sheer lace bralette and panties, she arched for a cigarette and snapped back, standing—a show horse on chrome legs, ready for her bath. Gallant, if just for the moment.

Innocent.

Trusting.

Any remaining equanimity that Dash clung to was being done in by the first-aid kit. He was one flustered son-of-a-bitch. If Reggie had been paying attention, she'd have noticed the humidity spike.

In the small zippered bag, he found a tube of Neosporin, burn ointment, and a bottle of alcohol, barely big enough to do the job. The top spun from his grip as if it was made of molten lead. Placing his hands on her taut thighs to steady her against the motion of the boat, he said, "This is gonna hurt."

"It's cool. I've been hurtin' for a long time now, Dash. I'm a pro." She blasted the smoke from her lungs. Her broad smile did little to hide her fear. The first splash felt like a flame-thrower. But—after that, it all went numb.

Again.

thirty

Exhausted from the ordeal of getting her wounds cleaned, Reggie was down for a better part of the afternoon. The sound of her arid throat crosscutting each breath filled the thick cabin with the song of misery whip-sawing its way through a giant sequoia. Her stomach, involuntarily raging in the absence of a manual over-ride, ached from the long night of tequila and nothing since.

Dash explored the boat's dank compartments and swollen drawers. A canvas bucket full of rusted pliers, scrapers, screwdrivers and a can of WD-40, almost rusted through at its bottom, were his rewards.

An old bleach bottle, dented pots and pans, several old winch handles, some usable lengths of line and, in a small drawer under the navigation desk, a once chromed ring of keys. Dash had hope that one would mate with the ignition portion of the instrument panel. Hope was just a fraction of what would be required to get that engine running, but it was basically all either of them had at the current moment.

With the sun past its zenith, and Reggie out on the settee, Dash stripped to his boxers. He fastened some of the quarter-inch line to a cockpit winch, and with rusted scraper in hand, lowered himself over the burnt stern into the cobalt blue water. The salt stung his gashes. He felt a slight pressure on his damaged chest cavity. The temptation to take mouthfuls was hard to resist.

With the island a low ripple on the horizon, Dash pondered the expanse of ocean that surrounded them. He permitted small ripples of fear to recapture hard won real estate in his mind. He thought about the emptiness gnashing his gut. The desert that was his mouth, lusted after the cool, clear, liquid. *You can't drink saltwater,* he thought, almost out loud. He had to stop thinking.

The coup d'état currently being waged by Dash's brain, interlaced with the real-life smell of the burnt fiberglass, began a twitching in his stomach. A tightness rose in his throat. Dry heaves. His mind needed to refocus—quick. With his body burning, he gulped as much air as his bruised lungs would allow and dove below.

***

When Reggie came to, she wasn't sure if the sound was in her dream or in the air surrounding her. Sore, but rested, she was in no rush to return from slumber. Then she heard it again, a heavy rasping against the hull, loud and terrifying. Her mind was brisk, well ahead of her body.

Was the boat in trouble? Had the gangsters from the dock finally found a way to reach them? Were they tangled in fish nets or—worst of all, run up onto a reef? She brought herself upright, and lunged for the companionway. "Dash?" she mumbled.

The adrenaline that kept the pain at bay all but vanished when she raised her leg to climb the ladder. "Dash!" The scream left her chest, louder than she'd intended. Reggie was doing exactly what everyone tells you not to do. She was panicking.

In the cockpit, there was no sign of him, just the horrific hammering on the hull. She scanned the horizon. Nothing but water. Throwing herself almost over the port side coaming, she gazed into the deep, crystal water, screaming at the top of her lungs; veins popping in her throat as all her fears screamed with her, "DASH!"

"What! Goddamn it. What?" Dash said, in a muffled voice.

"Where are you?"

"I'm down here." Like a blue crab, Reggie wriggled her way over to the starboard side. Peering, cautiously, to see a soggy Dash, floating.

"What the hell are you doing? You have busted ribs."

Dash chuckled and winced. "I scraped the bottom. The boat wouldn't sail with all that growth. You were sleeping. I needed a bath."

"That's not funny. You nearly gave me a heart attack."

"Sorry Reg— I needed to do something. Needed to stay busy. The inmates were starting to take over."

"How 'bout you get up here before you get eaten by a shark. If we don't eat, they don't eat."

"Roger that."

thirty-one

The sun rested itself on the infinite rim where the sea meets the sky and slowly began to deflate. Dash sat in his salt encrusted boxers, Reggie in her underwear.

Weary.

Thirsty.

Hungry.

"Dash, we have no food. No water. You realize that, right?"

"Yeah, Reggie. I realize that."

"What do you propose we do—starve?"

"No, Reg. I don't propose we starve."

To Dash, a decade had unfolded between the record release party and the present moment. In that time, humanity had lost the ability to endure. His humanity. He let his mind go to thinking. A sweet Georgia peach. Jules—one and the same. The tip of his nose softly

176

grazing the nape of her neck. Fresh like baby powder.

Reggie kept on. "Do you know where we're goin'? Do you know where we *are*? I mean...why can't we just turn around and go back? This shit's gotta be over by now?"

"We're not turning around. We don't know if that shit's over by now. I found some charts in the nav desk. I have an idea of where we might be."

Reggie was good in bed, great at sarcasm. "Hm. I feel so much better now. You have an idea of where we might be." She said, crossing her legs. "Terrific. I don't know why I was ever worried."

Dash struggled to sit up straight. He'd had about enough of all of it. "Reggie, I gotta say something." His ribs worse than before after his stint in the water.

"Dash—I'm sorry." Reggie cut him short. "I'm sorry I said that. I didn't mean to be a bitch." Her words machine-gunning. "I'm sorry I dropped the backpack. My dad's...Westie's ashes. I'm sorry I lost your wallet and shit—I'm just tired. I'm sore, and I'm fucking starving!"

"Reggie will you stop. Can you shut up, please? For one goddamn second...please." She didn't say another word. She sat back, smiled a tight smile and nodded.

"Thank you." Dash rubbed his hands through his salt stiff hair. "I don't care about the backpack. And, no—that's probably not how Westie wanted to go—bouncing down that road, but..." He caught himself. His gaze drifted; a soft buzzing of blimp motors in his head, to the apparition hovering over the boat. "Jesus Christ..." he whispered. "This was crazy. I'm not sure what I was thinking." Reggie remained silent. She startled when he snapped back and turned his gaze to her.

"Look, I don't know you. This—this here, wasn't part of the plan. You and me, we're here now—and we gotta make the best of it. What I do know is, you've been making life miserable for Westie for a long time." He stopped his words, wishing he could gather up the last few before they reached Reggie's inner ear. Dash's weir was dangerously close to crumbling. Whatever he'd been holding back for years appeared to be coming out right now.

"West—your dad...was a good man. Yes, he could have handled things differently. But things were crazy when your mom got pregnant. He was managing me...my shit took off...and—he just didn't have time..." Dash didn't finish the sentence.

"For what, Dash? A daughter?" Reggie said, with tears in her eyes. "He didn't have time for his fucking daughter...is that it?" Dash adjusted himself. His discomfort encroached. Reggie was an auger, carbide tipped. "Is this uncomfortable for you? You...asshole! My mom left me a handmade birthday card and three-hundred dollars on my sixteenth birthday. And then—split. She left me! Sixteen!" Reggie was standing in the cockpit, biting her thumbnail, heaving uncontrollably.

"My dad...had time for you! He had time for his asshole, rockstar client!" Reggie's gates released all that had been held back for years. The flooding of Miraflores was eminent. "Fuck you Dash! You have everything...and you don't even know it. The whole goddamn world at your feet." Dash starred off to the horizon. Drumming in his ribs, in his head. Dehydration and raw emotion landing their punches.

Reggie noticed the distance in his eyes. "What? You want me to shut up? Want me to shut up for 'one goddamn second?' My father—was a selfish asshole...who..." She choked on her tears. She could barely breath. "...cared more about you than he did me." Her last words tailed off. She had just then realized her truth.

Unable to avoid the onslaught, Dash coughed through the sob that was breaking in his chest. He stood up, with full eyes, to hug Reggie. He didn't get there. She pushed back from his advance, swung a wide open right hand which connected violently with the side of his head, in particular, his left ear. The force sent Dash crashing to the deck and Reggie clutching her aching hand.

Dash saw stars. A deafening feedback pierced his head. The throbbing now bedfellowed with nausea. The pain in his ribs was at its apex. They could ache no further. Reggie stood over him, trying to regain her composure. He shook his head; flexed his jaw muscles.

She just might have added a ruptured eardrum to the current list of maladies.

In one way, she hadn't meant to hit him so hard. In another, she hit him even harder. Her hand stung. The kind of sting that is almost indistinguishable from the sting that comes just before frostbite. This is the sting that brought the pigment to Reggie's eyes. She'd hit others before but, this might have been her best shot ever.

"Reggie," Dash said as he tried to sit up on the cockpit floor. "I'm sorry. Can you please...help me up?" Reggie bent to help Dash. When he reached for her, she retreated, ready for a retaliatory blow. She was tense, flexed, and her eyes wide. This young lady was used to full-contact discussions. She hadn't shown herself to be very adept at picking gentle men. Dash tried again, "I gotta tell ya something—about your dad."

thirty-two

When Jules turned her Rover onto Dash's street, she was two-thirds of the way to being a gelatinous mass. Exhausted from the drive to Hok'ee's ranch and the near immediate turn around, her brain flittered. Hot bath. Warm bed. Sensory deprivation, if only for a scant few minutes. There was only one task. Justice and Judge needed to be fed. She wasn't prepared for what she saw.

Jules landed hard on the brakes a quarter-mile shy of the turn-in to the driveway. The street was choked off. Cars pulled over haphazardly; bumpers in the weeds. News vans with satellite dishes extended high for a clear line of sight. Photographers with long lenses smoked and talked on cell phones. Camera crews readied tripods, leaned on audio booms and chatted nonchalantly—until the saw they Rover.

"Fuck," Jules said, snapping harshly into the present. They saw her. The cameras swung, boom ops pulled on their headphones. Coiffed news anchors hopped from air-conditioned vans and jostled for the perfect view point for their lead-ins.

Checking her rearview, Jules thought long and hard about slamming it into reverse. It was here. The story was out. How? She had no way of knowing. At least not from this vantage point. Adjusting her sunglasses, she drew a long, deep breath, and let her foot ease from the small square pedal to the long, rectangular one. The crowd surged as she approached.

She had to maintain speed. The worst thing that could happen was for her vehicle to come to a full stop. They would swarm. She'd never get going again. Photographers jammed the front of the truck, screaming, their dangling Canons and Nikons banging the front quarter panels.

"Mrs. Nelson! Jules—where's Dash?!" One reporter pointed a microphone at her closed window while jogging next to the coasting vehicle and yelled, "Was this a suicide pact? Have you spoken to Dash? Is he still alive?"

Jules hit the button on her visor to open the gate. She honked her horn and kept the truck coasting forward, gently nudging the brave paparazzi who dared get in front of the vehicle to shoot through the windshield. She checked her mirrors as the gates closed behind her. Relief to be inside would be delayed as all but one of the scumbags respected the gate. An overly enthusiastic soul in black jeans and the requisite photog shirt with an overabundance of pockets squeezed through at the last minute, trotting behind the truck as she accelerated up the driveway. Jules monitored him in the rearview. "Oh, you're gonna be so sorry," she said, as she pressed the button on her visor.

The garage door wasn't more than three feet into its ascent before the two lumbering K9s burst from underneath. They galloped to the Rover, tails wagging, tongues dangling; ears bobbing in anticipation to greet their doting mama. It took less than a second for their attentions to shift to the winded intruder cutting across the lawn.

Justice and Judge became missiles. Ears, once erect radar dishes, folded flat against their pointed skulls. The photographer turned so quickly when they emerged from the garage that he was in full stride towards the closed gate by the time they saw him. Cameras that once hung in precise order, now bounced and Charlie-horsed the middle of his back. Accessories darting from his body like fragments from an exploding dragster, he flailed desperately in retreat.

The dogs in full stride were thoroughbreds, neck and neck in silent pursuit. Jules thought about calling them off but resisted. This would send a message to the rest of the fuckers. Hopefully the cameras were rolling.

When the poor soul reached the gate, he was in mid-air. The ornate iron structure was six feet at the hinge with enough foot and hand holds to make it an easy climb. Easy is a relative term when two hundred-pound German Shepherds wanna tear your balls off.

With the photographer straddling the gate, one leg over, another still inside, Judge arrived. Letting out a gurgling, ferocious rumble of a bark, he launched straight up, eye-level with the fella. The photographer's expression was that of a man coming face to face with a violent demise. Photographers on the safe side of the action were snapping furiously. Cameras were indeed rolling.

Judge missed the photographer's terror-ridden face, but he did not miss entirely. He snapped down firmly on the dangling 5D that was collaring the man's neck. When gravity arrived, all one-hundred-and-twenty-five pounds of Judge's angst would most assuredly jerk the unfortunate bastards head clean off.

The cerebellum, the "little-brain," plays an important role in one's motor control. It contributes to cognitive functions such as language. It also regulates pleasure and, in this particular instance, fear responses. Its location, low on the base of the skull, was exactly where he felt the pressure from his camera strap. As it drew down tight, one would venture to bet the man on the fence now regretted purchasing the heavy-duty variety. Quickly, in one more millisecond, it would be too taut for him to draw out his head. Judge began to drift back down to terra firma.

The incident played out in the young man's favor. He escaped with his head, his balls, and all his other appendages. He crashed to the stone driveway, shit-soiled, minus one Canon 5D Mark III. Judge rendered it a merciless heap of mauled plastic, while Justice was raging at the gate. Photographers got close enough to get spewing spit on their lenses. The EF lens that Judge was mouthing was not so fortunate.

Quietly, Jules was glad the photographer made it. Relieved he wasn't disfigured. Both dogs turned instantly at her whistle. Judge dropped the 5D on the concrete garage floor at Jules feet. She extruded the small SD card from its saliva and dirt-covered slot. There was no dust door left to close. These photos would not be reaching their intended destination.

"Good boys," she said, tousling their ears once again, calming them down. "Can't wait to see the front page tomorrow," she said. Grabbing her overnight bag from the back seat, all three—Jules, Judge and Justice—entered through the kitchen.

thirty-three

In a span of just over forty-eight hours, Jules Nelson had driven the twenty-one hours from Nashville to Hok'ee's ranch and back again. Too much time to think on the road. Too many memories rearranging themselves on a timeline that had, until recently, been written in stone.

Sandstone.

The divorce was something neither of them wanted. It just seemed like the only alternative when the circus came to stay for a few days but never left. A certain velocity tends to overtake a great many things without much assistance, one being the planning of a wedding. Another being the conscious uncoupling of a couple. Divorce. Before they knew it, it happened. Now, they lived together. Separately.

Jules had the gate codes, alarm codes and keys to

everything that nobody else had. Fearing one day, she might accidentally walk in on him and a new lover, she decided to only let herself in when Dash was out of town. Even then, reluctantly.

She used the front of one boot against the back of the other and pulled up on her heel. Twice. Stranding her boots on the mat by the door, she tossed her keys on the island, as Dash had done many times and typed a hasty text. "Hey Charlie! I'm back. Thanks for watching the dogs. Gonna stay here tonight. Long drive. Love ya."

Two scoops of organic kibble, one for Justice. One for Judge. The double-door Sub-Zero was wasting its energy. Nine Heineken, a paper container of Lo Mein, two tubs of hummus, a half-gallon of almond milk and several types of gourmet mustard adorned the shelves. Two large bottles of Fiji water fit snugly in the door. She helped herself to one.

Clicking on the dimmers as she made her way hesitantly through the house, she sipped her water and listened to the silence. She glanced into the formal living room, where the huge couch sat, alone, as if in the center of Giants Stadium, adorned only in a Navajo throw, some pillows and one of Dash's custom Guilds. She started up the stairs, taking pause to notice the few photos on the wall as she ascended to the door of the bedroom.

An unfamiliar room to her. She picked out the

bedroom set at his request, but she and Dash had never made love in this house. It was the house *after* her. It served, as he said to her many times, "only to keep the rain off his head." She was afraid to look too closely. Afraid she might find another woman's underwear. Signs of a new body wash or shampoo for color-treated hair in the bathroom. She didn't linger. But nothing of the sort presented itself to her. There was nothing but the scent of Dash.

Justice and Judge hopped onto the bed, disregarding any stern reprimand they might have received the hundreds of times before. Jules sat on the edge of the mattress and surveyed the room, landing on the nightstand photo. It was of her and Dash, in his Mercedes, taken by Westie. Jules was draped over his shoulders, leaning from the passenger seat. She was kissing his cheek. Dash, with his favorite Ray-Bans on his forehead, smiling like he'd won the lottery. He had.

With Justice and Judge closely in tow, Jules made her way back downstairs to the bar, pondering the choices. To the dogs, she said, "Gentlemen...does mama want wine or a bit of the good stuff?" Deciding on the good stuff, she pulled down a tumbler, filled it with a handful of ice from the mini-fridge, and poured in a hefty measure of the 12-year. "Here's to your daddy," she said, replacing the cork and nudging the bottle back.

The dogs missed Dash. Their long, pink tongues

dripped a trail as they clung closely to Jules, and she made her way into the studio. The lights were on. The separate thermostat had the room at a brisk sixty-nine degrees. She smirked at the number—Dash did it on purpose. His childish profanity. She nudged the 'up arrow' to seventy-two and sat at the console.

Sipping on her Aberlour, she took it all in. Inhaled it. Let it seep deeply into the back of her throat. She felt the silence of that sanctuary. The soft-white overheads were dimmed midway. The tracking room looked as if Dash had just been there five minutes ago, excusing himself to the bathroom or outside to smoke.

His tobacco sunburst acoustic lay on the floor beneath the pair of SM-81s, and a single SM-7 vocal mic. A music stand contained his weapon of choice, a yellow legal pad, full of lyrics. A wooden stool on the side of his picking hand was speckled with guitar picks, two capos, a lighter and a mug. The scene was disquieting. He'd been plucked from the moment, without a trace. *He should be here*, she thought.

The console faders on channels 6 and 8 had been pushed up halfway. The "Master" fader was also at listening volume. The twin 21-inch monitors came to life when she nudged the mouse. A ProTools window showed three tracks, 3:41 of music—or something—had been recorded. She hit the 'return' key, then the space bar. She heard his voice almost immediately.

Dash always mumbled to himself when he was

recording his demos. Blathering on about the key or a possible second key of the song, a capo position or special tuning; verbal notes that he wanted to retain without having to write them down.

Jules sat back in lush studio chair and listened as Dash rambled. She could hear his rings and bracelet clack against the spruce top. She listened as he took a calming deep breath, as he always did, and became silent. All of his haphazard clumsiness ceased. A soft count; one, two, three, four, and a rhythmic strumming began. Just his bare fingers against the strings. When the vocal came in, she sat staring at the monitors, mesmerized as she had been a thousand times before.

> *Woke up this morning*
> *'bout half past three*
> *All the troubles I left behind,*
> *wouldn't leave me be*
> *You were lying there beside me, baby*
> *and the world was right*
> *All your naked warm surrender,*
> *I watched you dream all night*

She sipped her scotch, rubbed Judge's belly with her bare feet and played the song—over and over again. Just Dash and a guitar. His favorite way to deliver a song. Her favorite way to hear it. No production, no place to hide. He always said, "When you play it like that, you can't hide behind the band. It's just you and your song. And...you either are—or you aren't."

Somewhere in the beginning, middle or end of the fourth or fifth time through, her phone began to vibrate. She reached for it, not recognizing the area code. With Jules, if you weren't entered into her phone, you weren't anyone she wanted to talk with. But now, with the events of the past week, she was forced to answer all sorts of calls from all sorts of strangers.

She drew down the master fader on the console, "Hello?" An unfamiliar voice accompanied the unknown number. "Hello—Ms. Nelson?"

Jules confirmed, "Yes."

The male voice continued, "Ms. Nelson, this is Special Agent Watts. I'm with the FBI."

Jules felt the air suck from her chest.

"Ms. Nelson?"

thirty-four

Reggie rubbed her bare shoulders. Her almost-naked frame shuddered with a chill. Dash scanned the darkening horizon.

"Looks like we might get some weather." Reggie ignored him.

"What do you have to tell me?"

Dash wanted to postpone this discussion. "It's gonna have to wait. I gotta shorten sail and get this boat ready for an ass-kicking."

"Shit. Haven't we had enough ass-kicking?"

Dash brushed past her on his way to the mast. "It ain't up to me, Reg. This is how it goes out here. Once I reef these sails down, it'll be what it'll be. Hopefully, the old girl is strong enough to get us through the night."

Reggie spoke through cracked lips. "I'm so thirsty."

"Listen, if we get rain, it'll be a good thing. Go below and find something, anything to collect water."

As Reggie ducked below, Dash gazed again at the dense clouds and lighting strafing the sky. Any semblance of breeze was absent. The ocean's surface looked more like the undisturbed pool in his sorely-missed backyard. Deep azure water melted into an invisible horizon. "Calm before the storm," he said, stepping lightly into the cockpit. The first time he'd entered that way.

Below, he could hear Reggie rattling pans. He noticed the Clorox bottle on the nav station. She'd taken her job seriously. She'd done well. If only a rain squall, they'd feel much better after rehydrating.

From nothing to gale. Dash lay on the starboard settee, eyes closed, shielded in the crook of his left elbow. Reggie tucked up like a small duckling on her sail, dressed in a ratty t-shirt she'd shoved in her massive bag on the night of the riot. When the wind arrived, the boat heeled over instantly, throwing Reggie to the cabin sole.

Dash struggled to get off the starboard berth against the heel. He was first to the cockpit. The tiller was of little use now. The small piece of wood lashed to it would not bear the brunt of the leverage that would be placed upon it in foul weather.

He readied some line in an effort to keep it centered;

provide some resistance. Should it slam side to side in confused seas, it would quickly succumb and fail. Rudderless, they'd be doomed.

Dash yelled down to Reggie, "We're in it now! Here comes the rain." Reggie met him at the companionway, "I'm coming up!"

"No," Dash said, "Stay down there. Open that port in the head. The rain'll drip in pretty steady. Collect some pots...whatever. Fill 'em up. Drink it." Reggie made for the forward compartment. Unsteady, grasping for balance.

The downpour, so heavy and windblown, stung away any vision Dash might have had. On a port tack, the boat heeled to its gunwales. Dash huddled beneath the only protection they had from the elements. The crusty dodger did little to keep out the rain and served as a meek barrier to the wind.

Reggie was heaving. There was nothing coming except the few cups of water she just swallowed. "You okay?" Dash called to her. "No," she coughed. A steady stream of water trickled down the side of Dash's face. He tilted his head. The first of it tasted of salt. The salt from his hair. His face, his dry, cracked lips. Then it ran sweet. The soft, slight stream traced its way to his empty stomach, the hollow victor in an unfair fight.

3:40 am. That's what the Rolex was showing Dash's weary eyes. A glance below saw Reggie on the leeward side of the boat, wrapped in her sail, desperately fighting off the effects of full-blown seasickness. Pulsating eyes, an ache that transports one galaxies beyond any flu. Endless vomiting. Retching up nothing but gut. A quick death is all that one prays for in the grasp of the python. He was beginning to feel the thickness himself.

That once sweet rain pulsed from his guts. The cockpit drains overrun with the brackish mixture. "Maybe we should turn back," he said, not loud enough for Reggie to hear. Which way was back? He thought. There was no visual landmark. The seas had pushed them for hours. The compass swung wildly. There was no up, no down. No way to tell from whence they came. There was only one goal now; to survive the night.

With the storms intensifying, the seas grew. The tiller snapped at its lashing. They were out of control and turning broadside to the waves. When the boat crested the top of a swell, it would lurch over, almost to its spreader tips at the mercy of the gale force winds.

The gunshot pierced the darkness. Reggie shook from her self-induced coma. From below it sounded like a bomb dropped on deck. Dash peered over the aft end of the dodger in time to see the boom levitating. Lifting. Popping sail slugs from the track, one at a time. The goose-neck had given way. The front end of the aluminum boom was now set free and ripping the sail apart with reckless aplomb. Within seconds, the entire sail was free from the tack to the head. The halyard and topping lift were all that kept the assembly from flying off into the raging ocean. That would have been the best of all occurrences.

Dash ducked his head as the ten-foot long battering ram began its assault on the deck, making short work of the dodger. Reggie struggled to the companionway, arriving just as it splintered the companionway hatch with a second blow. "Stay down there!" Dash yelled. "This thing's gonna smash us to bits!" Reggie dove for the leeward settee. Dash couldn't hear what she was screaming.

The crash of the aluminum boom against the stainless shrouds was haunting. Piercing twangs, space age sounds of a metallic orchestra. The wind lifted the destruction high into the night sky. Dash prayed for it to break free at last. It wouldn't. The boom spun in a high arch, slow motion-like; the sail following like a well-trained dance partner. The whole assembly would careen into the deck, ricochet, then crash into the mast, shuddering the entire boat. Then it would repeat its attack.

With the leeward salon windows smashed through, rain and ocean entered at will. The boom completed its performance with a final pirouette into the starboard shrouds. With one faint swipe, the entire assembly swung through the gossamer like strands of wire and disappeared overboard. The flailing leeward shrouds tangled quickly in the remaining rig. Dash now pondered the decision to unfurl a sliver of headsail to keep the boat moving into the wind. His puckered hands cramped as the small line played out through his fingers.

The wind won. The line snapped. The entire headsail spun out. The wind filled it. The boat went over, heeled to the spreaders, Dash's tumbling body caught by the crumpled dodger structure. The warm ocean rushed in. The sweet rain gone. Salt water flushed his lungs. Any remaining strength presented itself as his hands clung the companionway. "Reggie!" She couldn't hear him.

The sweet little vessel was rolling over. When a rig under tension fails, the moment is swift. There's a pop, a silence, and then a crash. Dash heard none of it.

Part Three

thirty-five

Dash opened his eyes ever so slowly to small, cool droplets. A steady tapping of tiny, liquid feet tickled the decks. Unsure if he'd hopped the stick into the bosom of Abraham, he took several moments to assess the state of his rising and falling sternum.

The boat floundered silently under a low ceiling, not unlike an upside-down brandy snifter, full of smoke. Listing to starboard, her motion was stilted. Heavy. His limbs resisted any thought of movement. Gravity pressed him fast against the hard fiberglass coaming. Looking down the length of his body, he spotted his pink, pickled toes and thought the only thing missing was the toe tag.

He tried to wrestle himself upright, but abandoned the charge. His chest burned. What little breath he had whistled with the heat of a habanero. Purple and yellow bruises ran the length of his torso. His mind's eye envisioned a stack of busted popsicle sticks. Hands chafed raw from last night's battle waged and lost. After what seemed like consecutive hours, he felt himself upright, leaning hard with the angle of the boat. The sea was smooth, black marble.

In the opaque light, the damage was visible. Full effect. The boom had wreaked havoc on board. Chunks of gel coat were missing from where it impacted the hull and cabin top. The tempered glass in both salon windows had been smashed out with surgical precision. Those gaping voids allowed many gallons of sea to rush in when the boat rolled in the knockdown.

The whirling dervish was satisfied with such destruction, and before sailing off into the night's mayhem, took out the starboard side shrouds holding the stick vertical. When Dash unfurled the jib, the mast couldn't withstand the loads. It snapped off just below the spreaders. The whole rig—cables, mast section and tattered jib—was now dragging in the water alongside. The whole of the mess perilously close to sinking the small vessel. Dragging silently down, serpentine. Coming to rest at the feet of Davy Jones, like a feline drops the half-eaten blue jay.

Using the companionway, Dash cranked himself to a position that allowed him to peer inside. To Reggie. She lay as she had the entire day before. Fetal position, wrapped in her protective Dacron cocoon. Rain streaming in the blown-out salon ports. But something was drastically wrong. She lay with her eyes open. Still. Not moving. Dash felt panic. "Reg?" He moved to make his way down.

The cabin, again full to the knee, gently crested on the low side, inches below Reggie's mouth. Dash feared the worst. "Oh god, Reg...c'mon," he said, sloshing towards her. The moment he put his hand on her shoulder, she blinked at him.

Dash bent to her. She wasn't moving. "Reg—can you hear me?" He was staring into too-wide eyes. "Reggie. Please kid...say something." Her cold, grey skin had surrendered all its heat. Her eyes blinked and her lips wanted to move. "Oh no, no, no," Dash said now realizing her hypothermic state.

He peeled away the wet sail and climbed behind her on the settee. He pressed his frame to fit her identical shape. Spooning on the saturated bunk. "C'mon kiddo," he said. "I need ya. Don't go fading on me now." He rubbed furiously at her shoulders and arms. His feet rubbed against her feet. Frantically, he tried to get his body heat to warm her; coax her organs back from the brink.

After all the hours baking in the molten sun, they had their rain. The liquid of life, dripping from every orifice, and he prayed for the sun.

thirty-six

The white Rover turned onto Hillsboro Road, headed for 1st Avenue.

"Good morning kid. How's it going out there?"

"Hi, Gary. It's a circus."

"I'm sorry. Want me to send an officer?"

"No need. They're already there. One at the end of the road and one at the gate."

"Okay. Any word from Dash?"

"No," Jules said. "Nothing. I'm freaking out. Sorry—I know that's not very stoic, but neither Hok'ee nor Charlie have heard anything, either. I tried to call Cholo's place but the call won't go through. Some crap about 'experiencing difficulty' et cetera, et cetera."

Gary chuckled. "You can freak out, Jules. You're allowed. I'm worried myself. To make matters worse, I had a visit from a friend at the FBI the other day."

Jules cut him short, "Watts!"

"Yes," Gary paused. "Special Agent Watts. You know him?"

"No. But that's why I'm calling. I'm meeting him at Dose. I'm on my way right now. I'm not sure what to say, Gary. I'm a basket case. I'm not a good liar."

Gary tried to calm her down. "Jules...there's nothing to lie about. There's been no crime. We aren't even sure what happened. And we won't be until Dash gets home. Just be you. Be Jules. He'll do what every other man on the planet does. He'll immediately fall in love with you!"

"Thanks Gary...that doesn't help," she said. "I'm being serious. I'm—scared. I don't do well with authority figures."

"Okay, Jules. I'm sorry." Gary changed his tone. "If we're being serious, I gotta ask you a question." Pausing, knowing what he was about to ask could make Jules even more nervous. "Before he went off on this half-cocked adventure of his, Dash gave me three-hundred-thousand dollars in cash. Do you know anything about that?"

Jules was completely confused. "Three-hundred thousand dollars? No. I have no idea..."

Before she could finish the sentence, her phone pinged in her ear. "Hang on Gary," she said, glancing at the screen. Her Twitter app alerted her to a direct message. The message was from Cholo. "Gary, it's

Chooch. I gotta call you back." She didn't listen for him to hang up.

Jules jerked the Rover into the parking lot of Howlin' Books to read the message. She felt a full-fledged panic attack coming as she read Cholo's message.

ISLAND ERUPTED. RIOTS. NO WAY 2 CALL. AIRPORT SHUT DOWN. CAN'T FIND D. SORRY TO TWEET.

Jules typed with lighting speed.

THNX CHOOCH! HAVEN'T HEARD A WORD FROM HIM. WORRIED! CALL WHEN U CAN. BE CAREFUL.

She hit the redial to Gary's office. All eight cylinders pumped maximum horsepower as she spun the Michelins through the yellow light.

Watts' figure looked more like a Ken doll than that of the far-reaching FBI agent she expected. Setting the hand brake with a hefty tug, she shoved the door and kept it ajar with an extended, deliciously stiff leg. Hopping from the truck, she let the weight of the door carry it to its latch.

"You must be Agent Watts." She said, with an extended hand.

"And you must be Ms. Nelson."

"Call me Jules."

"Okay, Jules. Can I buy you a cup of coffee?"

"Actually, Agent Watts, I'm afraid I won't be able to stay for coffee."

"I don't understand. You agreed to meet. You picked the time. The place."

"I know. I'm sorry but something's come up. I can't stay."

"Ms. Nelson, I've been stonewalled on every front by your people. Gary Smith, Charlie Tate—and now, you. This is not going to get easier, only more difficult. At some point, the snare is going to trip. It's just a matter of whose feet will be in it."

"Agent Watts, I don't wish to be rude or waste your time, but I don't know anything. Since you've already spoken to *my people*, Gary and Charlie, I would venture to say, you know more than I do at this point."

"Jules...tell me about the money." Watts eyed her reaction. Her body language. Jules didn't blink. She didn't fidget. She made sure to catch Watts squarely in his deep, blue eyes.

"I don't have any idea about the money. And, honestly...I couldn't care less. I'm trying to find my husband, Mr. Watts. Dash...Westie...they were decent men. If there's a substantial amount of money that's raising some questions for the FBI, I'm certain there's a credible explanation."

"Well ma'am. I hope you're right. I sure hope it isn't your pretty little size sevens swinging from that bough."

How much time would have to be served for clocking a federal agent with a stiff right hand? The image flashed like a glint of sunlight from a chrome bumper, but she let it flutter off into the morning shadows.

"On that note, Mr. Watts, you have a nice day." Jules chuckled. She descended the deck steps with a soft grace, careful not to stomp her heels into the stair treads. The key fob clicked under a French-manicured thumb. Automatic locks released the doors with a flash of the headlights. Before she relaxed her leg to let the door close, she chirped to Watts who eyed her from the deck. "Any further requests can go through my attorney. I believe you've met."

The blood was rushing to Watt's head faster than he'd counted on. The arteries in his eyes would soon bulge past their capacity and hemorrhage. He could almost hear the change cascading from his pockets as he bounced helplessly, entangled in his own snare.

thirty-seven

The brief intellectual jousting match with Watts left Jules seeking refuge. A quick jaunt to the yoga studio and a drop in for an unscheduled massage reset her polarity, which lasted all of thirty minutes. Two photographers ambushed her as she left Whole Foods. With groceries in hand, Jules had to squeeze past the reporter's microphone, into the tight space between her truck and the Panera Bread van. She lingered at the door, fumbling for the keys as their shutters clicked, capturing her non-responses. The female reporter peppered her with inquiries until Jules finally craned the door open. The engine roared and the Rover backed with little regard for anyone in close proximity. "Goddamn it." She said to herself. "So much for Savasana."

Every turn the Rover made, the two pursuit vehicles

made as well. Jules' eyes fluttered between the road ahead, the rearview, and the speedometer. Grasping for her cell, she dialed Gary Smith again.

"Hey, Jules."

"Gary...I'm sorry—I'm being followed."

"Followed? Where are you?"

"I just left the market. That woman from channel five ambushed me in the parking lot. It could be them. Watts? FBI? I have no idea."

"Okay, Jules. Go to the house. I'll call the Major. He'll arrange more security."

"Gary, I don't want guards at the house. I have the dogs. The cops are out front. It already feels like I'm under siege."

"Any more from Chooch?"

"No."

"Go home, Jules. Take a hot bath. This is not going to calm down anytime soon, I'm afraid. Call me if you need me."

The officer waved Jules through the gate with little fanfare. Cameras flashed and the din was muffled outside the vehicle. She couldn't help but notice the crowd had doubled. She focused forward and made swift to the garage.

CNN reverberated through the house, mixing with the whines and busy paws of the two pups. Jules grabbed a water from the fridge.

"The bizarre case surrounding music star Dash Nelson seems to be getting stranger every day..." She didn't need to hear another word. She quickly grabbed the remote and hit the mute button. The television screen was ablaze with photos of Dash and Westie. Misinformed banners scrolled across the screen every few seconds:

DASH NELSON DISAPPEARANCE

MANAGER'S STOLEN BODY STILL MISSING

FOUL PLAY SUSPECTED: POSSIBLE SUICIDE PACT

"Jesus Christ...you fucking assholes," Jules let slip. Peering through the sheer curtains to the street, she could see two Metro Police cars. Their seizure-inducing flashes over-emphasized the situation.

The totem that was Dash's past was casting a long shadow over the present. As the meteorite travels through the sky, its relationship with the sun changes, thereby changing the shadow cast. Jules feared that shadow might grow long enough to touch the future.

Justice and Judge laid on the floor by Jules feet, attentive to her moves; her words. "How we gonna sleep through this?" She said, opening her laptop.

Google
Bonacca Riots

She skimmed the reports about the uprising on Bonacca. She read about the efforts of a few deep-pocketed developers to force the islanders' hands. It worked. The uprising gave them permission to use force. The force, as it usually does, met with resistance. And—somewhere in all of that, was Dash.

Jules grabbed her phone and opened her Twitter app. She messaged Cholo.

CHOOCH - ANY WORD? PLEASE CALL

Fifteen minutes later, Jules's phone vibrated.

"Hello?"

"Jules—"

"Chooch! Oh my God. Are you okay?"

Cholo's voice was distant, the connection weak. "Jules, I'm on a satellite phone. Don't have much time. Things here not good, luv...island gone crazy. Cholo's still standing. Listen—my people say Dash and Reggie tried to get south. Didn't make it. They say he on a boat!"

Jules cut in. "Wait...who's Reggie? On a boat?"

Cholo didn't give her a chance to say more. "Reggie! Dey on a boat. God help them tonight. Bad storm here, girl. Honduran Navy...rescue boats...they been told. But dey ain't goin' out der tonight—"

The call dropped. Jules slammed her phone into the couch. "Ugh!" She searched her memory. She grasped at every morsel of spoken word floating in the atmosphere trying to remember any mention of such person. "Reggie? On a boat? Oh Dash, what've you done?" Jules looked up to the muted TV just in time to see the banner scrolling across the CNN screen:

RECORD SALES & DOWNLOADS SOAR...
HEAVY CLUTCH IN HEAVY ROTATION

She unmuted the story to catch the tail end. Her gaze returned to the laptop. She logged in to Dash's Twitter page and couldn't believe what she was seeing. Eight million followers! She logged in to Facebook, the posts on his page were endless. Social media was ablaze.

Trending:
#dashnelson
#paulwest
#deathpact

It was no longer too early for a drink. She released a cold Heineken from the door and trotted up the steps to the bedroom with Justice and Judge at her hips. Through the window she had a better vantage to the street. Peeling back the curtain, she cracked the window open a few inches. People were playing acoustic guitars and singing Dash Nelson songs. News anchors, reporters and self-proclaimed journalists crammed microphones and cell phones in people's faces. Camera flashes were popping off every few seconds, capturing moments. Any moments. However misshapen they happened to be. She hit the speed dial for Gary Smith. It went straight to voicemail.

thirty-eight

Justice and Judge spread liberally across the king-sized bed, Jules resigned to a small sliver on the edge. The streetside serenade made its way up to the bedroom in the still of the night. The last glimpse of the clock read 4:30am before she finally fell away from it all. When she grabbed her cell to douse the alarm, it was only 7am. Her sleep was restless at best.

In his bed, bareback, she let his smell caress her entire body beneath the sheets. Dash was on her. She didn't know where he was in the world, but on this morning, he was front and center in her psyche.

She changed her mind on the way to the shower, tugged her snug jeans up over her hips, and slipped into one of Dash's well-worn denim shirts. She pulled in his essence and shooed the lazy dogs from the bed. "Your daddy's gonna kill me when he sees the dog hair on this bed."

The three of them went to the kitchen. Jules put on a pot of coffee and let the dogs out the back door. A small fenced in area around the pool made sure they couldn't get to the front gate. And, more importantly, made sure the front gate couldn't get to them. When they finished their morning deposits, she hailed them for breakfast. Their usual organic dry kibble was spruced up with two scrambled eggs. Jules always spoiled the dogs.

The sweet aroma of the brewed beans perked her spirits. She fixed a smoothie, put a teaspoon of organic honey in her coffee and took up residence at the kitchen table. The MacBook chime raised her heart rate a tad. She feared the morning news. Her thoughts went to the storm in Bonacca last night. Reggie. Why doesn't she remember Dash ever mentioning a Reggie?

Gary answered on the first ring. "Hello Jules," he said, "Things have gotten a bit interesting around here, huh?"

"Interesting's a good word. Have you seen the news?" she said.

"Oh yeah, I've seen it. You have an impromptu carnival out there, it appears."

"Yeah, they're behaving for the most part. 'Cept for one fella who about shit his pants when he slipped through the gate and tried to get to the house."

Gary guffawed. "I bet that fella's questioning his life choices about now." They both had a hearty chuckle.

Jules brought it back to the real reasons for her call. "Gary—has anyone checked the latest numbers on *Clutch*? CNN is reporting brisk sales and heavy rotation. Did radio jump on board?"

"I've checked the numbers. Since the story broke, he's passed gold. Five-hundred thousand and counting. Country radio, rock radio—Europe's blowing up. Hell, even college and non-comms are all over it. I've been trying to field the calls. I have Westie's cell phone. It's been a little nuts."

"You know they're saying crazy stuff. TMZ. CNN. Death pacts? Where'd they get this shit? Some reports say he's dead."

"Listen, Dash ain't dead. I know what they're saying. These days, it's about being first to air. It ain't about getting it right. Sensationalism leads. I've had four calls from Anderson Ellis at CNN wanting an interview. Fallon, Colbert, Fox and NPR."

Jules was shocked, "Holy shit, Gary. This is insane. I got a call from Cholo, he said the island rioted. The airport is closed. He also said Dash is on a boat with someone named Reggie. Who's Reggie?"

"On a boat? Where in God's name..." He tried to grasp what Jules said. "Reggie? I don't know of anyone named Reggie. But Jules, I've never been down there. That was Dash and Westie's secret spot. No telling what the hell they got into down there."

"I know," Jules said.

"Get back to this boat stuff. What did Cholo say?"

"He said they were on a boat. He said he contacted the Honduran Navy and rescue boats, but they couldn't get out last night because of weather. Bad weather."

"Last night! You had this conversation last night? Why didn't you call me?" Gary was furious.

"I did. It went straight to your voicemail."

"Well, shit...let me jump off here. I'm gonna call the Coast Guard. Have you got a way to reach Cholo?"

"I called the Coast Guard when I couldn't reach you. The information Chooch gave was so vague...they said they'd be in touch. I've tried the satellite number he called me from, but it didn't go through."

"Keep trying," Gary said. "I'll call you back when I know something." Gary hung up without letting Jules respond. She tried the satellite number again. Nothing. She opened Twitter and typed another message to Cholo.

CHOOCH - NEED TO TALK. CALL ME!

Jules' phone vibrated on the table.

ALLIE HART

"Allie!" Jules said.

"Hey girl. How you holding up?"

"I'm good. Worried. Terrified...there's a circus in the

218

driveway. You know...good."

Allie chuckled, "I can't imagine, Jules. I really can't. I'm watching the news and—the bullshit that's being said. Who's running interference for you guys?"

"Gary's fielding most of the calls, but I'm gonna jump in and take over."

Allie was stern. "Jules—you can't do that. You need a professional. One point person. Gary can't do it. He's got his hands full. They're about to overflow when the legal stuff starts to fly. You shouldn't do it. You're the wife...ex-wife." She checked her words. "You know what I mean. You're too close. They'll eat you alive. Let me do it. I'll call Gary. I'll have Westie's cell number forwarded to my number and I'll field the calls." Allie was a pro's pro.

Precise.

Efficient.

Fiercely loyal.

Nobody crossed her. Not more than once, anyway.

"Allie, you're a godsend. I don't know what I'd do without you."

"I love you, Jules," Allie said. "We'll talk later."

Relieved for the moment, Jules opened a weather page and searched for Bonacca. While the page loaded, she sipped the remains of her tepid coffee. The headline made her choke:

TROPICAL DEPRESSION RIPS RIOT-TORN BONACCA

thirty-nine

A gentle tapping is what stirred him. A rounded thud; a rubber mallet sounding a parquet floor. Again, he tried to assemble the pieces of the latest puzzle. This time, inside the boat. This time, with a body pressed against his busted trestle. He remembered Reggie. He couldn't believe he'd fallen asleep.

Laying on his right side, the arm under him ablaze with pins and needles, he put his left arm over Reggie and felt her chest. The center, just between her breasts, bare and firm with bone. He felt the light thumping of her heartbeat. He felt a warmth that was missing before. He pressed his lips into her damp hairline. He could feel her pulse.

She tasted salty.

She was warm.

He whispered, "Reg."

She slowly turned into him. He did his best not to wince. "Welcome back," he said.

She was confused. "What?" She was trying to focus her eyes. Trying to assemble different pieces to the same puzzle. "What the hell...I feel like shit."

Dash was pressing against her back, keeping her weight off his ribs. "You've had quite the couple-a-days," he said.

She pulled herself upright, "Me? What about you?" She glanced around at the faltering boat, "Man, this boat is trashed. I can't believe we aren't freakin' dead."

Dash extended his hand, "Can you help me up?" She gently tugged. Dash was in serious pain, "Ow, easy...easy." Reggie studied the whole scene. The sun began to poke through the outer bands of the storm. The boat was warm.

"Dash, we can't stay out here another night. We gotta get you to a hospital."

"I know, Reg." Dash felt responsible for their predicament. "Listen, I'm sorry. We shoulda turned back. This boat wasn't..."

Reggie cut him off. "Bullshit. We couldn't go back. It's not your fault. Well, maybe it is your fault but...we're still here. We're alive, kinda."

Dash chuckled. "Thanks, Reg. That was one hell-of-a pep talk. You ever think of goin' pro?" She laughed. Searching her purse, she pulled out a pack of American Spirits. Dash's eyes lit up.

The pack was saturated. She peeled it open and laughed. "We can set 'em in the cockpit! The sun'll dry 'em out."

Dash smirked. "We gotta bail this water out. We gotta cut them cables and let that mast go or it'll punch a hole, pull us right to the bottom."

Reggie nodded. "Okay—but you ain't allowed to help. You gotta just sit—rest. You die out here and I'm gonna be pissed."

Before she could scoop a single bucket's worth of water, her expression changed. She cocked her head; focused like she was figuring out a tricky algebra formula. "Dash—do you hear that?"

Dash shook his head, "No. I don't hear..."

Reggie interrupted, "Shh!" She stood up to peer out the salon ports. "You don't hear that? That—hum?"

Dash's eyes got wide, "Reggie, a 'hum' isn't a good thing in the middle of the ocean. Help me up!"

She was first to the companionway. "Holy shit! It's a boat!"

Dash crammed himself behind her on the same step of the ladder. "No shit." He wasn't sold on the idea that it was not a mirage.

Reggie was elated, jumping up and down in the slanted cockpit. "Holy shit! Holy shit! HOLY...SHIT! Dash...aren't you happy?!"

"Yeah, Reg. I'm ecstatic. I just ain't sure yet if I'm seeing what I think I'm seeing."

"Of course you are, you crazy bastard. That...is a fuckin' boat. And it's coming straight at us!" The moment struck them both at the same time.

"They see us, right? Dash...they—see us."

"I sure hope so." Dash ducked below and found the canister of expired flares. He had stowed it high in the driest cubby for such a moment, should it ever present itself.

The boat was closing fast. Growing larger on the horizon each minute. Dash pulled the small plastic flare gun from the bright orange canister and loaded a shotgun-sized shell into the chamber. Reggie squinted and plugged her ears with her index fingers.

"Those things gonna work?"

"We'll see," he said, clicking the flimsy chamber closed. With arms extended at an imaginary point in the sky, he squeezed the trigger.

CLICK.

CLICK.

"Shit. Shells musta got wet." He released the shell and reset it, again, aiming in the direction of the approaching vessel.

CLICK.

CLICK.

Nothing.

Dash tried several shells. Each one yielding the less than stellar "click." The approaching vessel was on them, bow high and steaming full speed ahead. *They gotta see us...they have to fuckin' see us*, Dash thought, raising the gun with yet another incendiary candidate. Aiming straight ahead now, a vice cop with a perp dead to rights, he squeezed.

CLICK.

"Fuck me!" Dash slammed the gun on the cockpit coaming. "You gotta be kidding me!" Reggie ducked for a place to hide. He was coming unglued. Dash's hair fell in his gaunt face. His wide eyes focused once more. With arms extended, he squeezed. "C'mon you piece-a-shit."

BOOM!

The flare launched. A blaze of red flame. A burst of sulfur in the nose. Its graceful arc headed straight for the bridge deck, then dipped and fell short, disappearing into the bow wake. "Goddamn it!" Dash gushed, "Gimme another one."

Reggie fumbled for another shell, but they scattered like marbles. She couldn't discern which pile was the flares already tried, and which were untried.

"Reg?!" Dash didn't take his eyes off the boat. The massive, steel vessel was now just a couple hundred yards away, the windshield disappearing behind the bow. Dash barked, "Reggie! Give me a goddamn shell!"

"Okay!" she thrust her best option into his palm. He couldn't get it seated correctly. He was rushing. Doing what they always tell you not to do—panicking. He drew a deep breath and clicked the shell into the housing. Again raising his arms, he had one more chance. He closed his eyes and whispered, "C'mon baby." Squeeze.

BOOM!

The red flame shot from the barrel and careened into the pilothouse windshield. Sparks erupted and cascaded around the decks. Reggie burst out, "You hit 'em! Dash...you hit 'em!"

"Yep. I hit 'em. But they ain't stopping."

"Should we jump?"

"Naw...the props'll chew us up like chum."

"What do we do?" Reggie was wide-eyed, flustered. Dash tossed the gun overboard, and said, "We pray."

If Dash and Reggie had been floating in a particular section of the sub-Arctic ocean instead of the Western Caribbean, a decent sized Beluga just might have fit in the gaping hole that was Reggie's mouth.

forty

A hundred yards. Closing. The bow suddenly dipped. The stern of the steel vessel rose as the wake caught up and passed under. Dash and Reggie prepared for the same wake to rock them.

"Hola, señor!" A voice blasted from a crackling loudspeaker. "Señorita! Estamos aquí para ayudar!"

The clunking diesels chugging black smoke nudged the imposing bow closer to the small sailboat. Neither Dash nor Reggie were certain this was really happening. A second later, the loud speaker came alive again, slaying any doubt. Almost too loud to be discernible, came the opening chords to *Heavy Clutch*. Dash knew the chords. He smiled that million-dollar smile that hadn't been smiled in quite some time. He laughed so hard he doubled over. The guffaw turned into heaving coughs, which produced bloody, red mucus.

Reggie was seated in the cockpit. "Are you kidding me? You have to be fucking kidding me." She turned to Dash, "That's you? That's your music?"

Dash, with hands on his knees, grinned ear to ear. "Yep. That's me. Course, that speaker's a little mid-heavy. The record sounds much better."

Reggie shrugged, "Of course it does."

The SACRED MARIE drifted alongside, the ship's captain at the rail with a smile to rival Dash's big grin. Light rain ran over the rail in tiny brackish waterfalls darkening the rusty hull.

"Hola! Dash Nelson! Heavy Clutch...beeeg fan! We all beeeg fan!" Several dark-skinned crew gathered at the rail as well. Dash waved.

"Hola Capt'n, de donde eres?"

"Honduras!" The captain of the Sacred Marie went on, "Señor Dash, Amedica think you dead!"

Reggie reacted. "What? Did he say America thinks you're dead?"

"Yeah..." Dash laughed, "I think that's what the man said."

The captain shouted to his crew, "Dash Nelson not dead! Dash Nelson on my boat! Sagrada Marie! No puedo creer esto!"

Dash said, to no one in particular, "Me either amigo. I can't believe it, either."

Reggie, chin in her hands, firmly in the grip of her exhaustion thought, *In the middle of the goddamn ocean? Of all the people who could have rescued us, we have to get rescued by a ship full of Dash Nelson fans. Honduran Dash Nelson fans? There'll be no living with him.*

The rope ladder crashed down on the slanted deck. Dash turned and extended his hand to Reggie. "My lady—your chariot awaits."

"You're not funny, you know." Reggie took his hand. "Sometimes I wanna..."

Dash interrupted, "Punch me? You already did that. How about you just get on the boat Reg?"

forty-one

When Allie Hart suggested that the only way to properly combat the mendacious social media storm was for her to go prime time, Jules had serious regrets about discontinuing her Xanax prescription, for interviews of any kind were on the list—one notch above root canals and pap smears.

With Dash's studio lit dramatically, Jules Nelson sat directly across from CNN's Anderson Ellis. The soft white light from the Keno Flo created tiny stars in her pupils. The makeup girl finished her last looks and Allie Hart stood off camera by a monitor, at the ready for her friend.

While Anderson finished his opening, Jules prayed the moisture, any moisture, would return to her mouth. She crossed her legs calmly and listened for her cue. "Jules Nelson. Thanks for allowing me to come here—

and for talking. I know it's a difficult time."

"It's been a little crazy, Anderson."

"First things first. As we understand it, at this point in time, Dash Nelson, your former husband, is alive and well?"

"He's alive, yes. Well? That's a loaded question." She smiled to inject some levity.

Anderson returned the gesture. "This story seemed to go from zero to one hundred in almost no time. TMZ first reported on this about 48 hours ago and now social media is blowing up all over the world. You have news teams and fans camped in your driveway. How are you handling all the attention?"

"Yeah, It's a bit of a carnival at the house, but we're good."

"Okay—you're going to have to connect the dots for us. Let's go back a little over a week ago, when Paul West, Dash's longtime manager and close friend, passed suddenly. And, let me say, I'm sorry for your loss. I've known you all for many years, I know what Paul West meant to this family."

"Thanks, Anderson."

"Friday morning, Paul West is found dead. Friday night, Dash visits him at the morgue. When the attendant returns, Dash and the body of Paul West are gone. Early Saturday morning, an Oklahoma State Trooper confirmed stopping Dash for speeding. He also confirmed the body of Paul West was in the back of the vehicle. There's speculation as to where he was headed. There have been reports of a death pact. Can you speak to any of this?"

Jules could feel the blood rush to her face. "Well, there was no death pact, I can tell you that. The internet has been quite frantic with the wild fantasies and speculation. Westie died from a suspected heart attack. There was never a single mention of foul play, and any suggestion of suicide is absolutely absurd. All anyone knows for certain, at this point, is that Dash is alive." She tried not to shift her weight. Allie was fixated on the monitor.

"A big story this week has also been the situation on the island of Bonacca. Reports of civil uprising and a tropical storm. Dash was on that island." Raising his finger, "If I may continue. One source said he stole a boat and sailed directly into the path of that tropical storm. Today, we received word a Honduran research vessel pulled him from a sinking sailboat in the South Water Caye Marine Reserve, fifteen miles from the coast of Belize. I mean, Jules...this sounds like a Hollywood movie script, does it not?"

Jules smiled nervously, "Allegedly...allegedly stole a sailboat."

Anderson laughed, "Of course. Allegedly...my apologies."

"It does sound a bit fantastical. Hollywood is a good word. But...I haven't spoken to Dash yet. I have no idea what happened after he left us all at the hospital that day Westie died. People have gone crazy with all sorts of preposterous scenarios. Yes, Dash was on Bonacca when it erupted. I have no idea why he was there. A Honduran research vessel did pull him from a sailboat."

"There was a second person pulled from the sailboat with Dash. Do you know who that person is?"

Jules swallowed hard, "No, I don't."

"I understand your lawyers have advised you not to talk about the specifics but, in the interest of due diligence, I have to ask. Are you worried? I mean, there will be, I would expect, a lengthy investigation. A body is missing. Your former husband has been directly connected to that body. Allegedly, that body was driven cross-country."

Anderson paused, then folded his hands over his note pad. "There are so many things going on with this case, Jules. Another report has Dash connected to a very large sum of money being transferred out of the country. Has the FBI contacted you?"

Jules dreaded the question. She sat upright and looked directly into Anderson Ellis's eyes, "The FBI has been in contact, yes. Dash and Westie were honest men. If either one is connected to that money, I'm sure there's an explanation. I won't speak any more on that." She blinked. Composed herself. She needed to shift the focus of this interview.

"Anderson, we've lost a dear member of our family this week. Until a few hours ago, we were preparing for possibly more bad news. We didn't know if Dash was alive or dead. The Coast Guard has informed us that he has been rescued. There's a protocol that needs to be followed. When they bring Dash home, we'll know more. I'm waiting just like all of you, for a story that only Dash can tell."

Jules didn't give Anderson the opportunity to ask another question. "Our music family, our friends and our fans...lost a big part of ourselves this past week. We haven't been able to properly grieve for Westie. We need to be allowed to do that. I'm asking people to respect that wish."

The interview was over.

As the crew packed up, Anderson hugged Jules, "I'm sorry this is happening. You know I'm a fan...and a friend."

"I know, Anderson. Thanks."

Allie Hart pulled Jules aside. "Hey. I know that was hard. Now that Dash has been rescued, you don't need to say anything else. That was your statement, the closing, by the way, was incredible."

"Thanks, Allie."

"You know, when he gets home, this mess is going really explode."

"I know," Jules said.

"Okay," Allie gathered up her things, "I'm gonna

leave with the camera trucks if you're cool? This way, the gate opens once, and I don't get trapped."

"No problem."

Jules' phone vibrated. "Hello?" An unfamiliar voice spoke in quick blasts. "Ms. Nelson, this is Petty Officer Henry, United Stated Coast Guard. Ma'am, we've been in contact with Captain Hernandez aboard the Sacred Marie. Your husband has undergone a medical evaluation. Minus some dehydration, some cuts, bruises, and a few fractured ribs, he seems to be fine. It's my understanding you'll be receiving a satellite call anytime now."

"Thank you, Officer Henry, I appreciate the call."

"You're welcome ma'am. You have a good night."

How ironic, Jules thought. 'You have a good night.' Sounds so simple.

forty-two

Dash stared for a moment at the buttons on the sat phone. The sleek, black box of space-age tech was to shoot a beam up into the Milky Way, bounce it off a glorified trash can lid, straight into the lap of consequence. There were only a handful of phone numbers he remembered by heart: West, Gary, Charlie, and Jules. Squinting, an arm's length away, his fingers mashed the soft silicone buttons.

"Hello?" Jules answered, cautiously.

"Hey honey...I'm gonna be a little late for dinner."

"Anyone ever tell you what an asshole you are, Dash?"

"Yeah, my ex-wife."

"Smart woman."

Dash avoided the seriousness. "What'd I miss?"

"Well," Jules said, as if glancing over a grocery list

quickly scribed on the back of her dry-cleaning receipt. "Let me look at my notes." She could hear the puff of air in Dash's smirk. "Half the world thinks you're dead. The other half thinks your psychotic. You're wanted by the FBI. There's about a hundred and fifty people living in your driveway, and the grass needs to be cut. Oh, and...*Heavy Clutch* is number one."

Dash paused, wondering if he heard correctly, "Goddamn. I guess I shoulda let Calvin know I was leaving town. That yards a bitch to cut when it goes too long."

"Dash," Jules said, "Can you stop being a jerk-off for a second?"

"Sure."

"We've been going out of our minds around here. Worrying—wondering what the hell was going on."

Dash cut her off. "Jules, it's not the time."

"I know—I know it's not the time to discuss this! I get it." She calmed herself, "You're safe. That's what matters. But goddamn it Dash. What the..." Jules stopped herself. For the moment, her dainty finger plugged the geyser, postponing the hydrothermal explosion until a more appropriate time. Like when she could actually get her hands around his throat.

"Who's Reggie?"

"Reggie—is Paul's daughter."

He heard the gasp of air through the satellite line. "What?" Jules was stunned. "West has a daughter?

You—never told me?"

This realization struck Dash in a weird place. He swore there was a logical explanation as to why Reggie had needed to be kept a secret, but that logic alluded him at the current time.

"Listen, It's a long, crazy story. I'll tell ya everything when I see ya. I promise."

"It's gonna be a shit-storm when you get home. Tim's offered to send his plane. I accepted."

"Okay, tell him I said thank you. He's a hell of a guy."

Her silence said it all. Dash continued. "Jules, I know it hasn't been easy on you. I'm sorry I left you hangin'..."

Jules cut in. "How could you not tell me about West's daughter? You've never...kept secrets." She stopped that thought. A pregnant pause bearing the weight of triplets. "Look, I guess... I'll see you when you get here."

The connection went to space and back. Jules felt every bit of distance. Alienated. Estranged from the man she thought she knew better than anyone else on the planet.

"Hey," he said, hoping she hadn't hung up yet.
"Yeah?"
"How are the dogs?"
"They're fine." She said, letting a light chuckle escape. "They almost got themselves a photographer for dinner. I think the poor guy shit his pants going over the wall."

Dash laughed out loud. Then, he got up the nerve to ask the question. "Is *Clutch* really number one?"

"Yeah—your record is really number one," she said, squeezing her lips together. The way she does when she puts on her lipstick.

"Well—shit. Wish I could tell West." Dash sniffed.

"He knows," she said. "Get some rest. You're gonna need it."

forty-three

The Sacred Marie secured her lines at the Glover Reef Research Facility just before 5:00 PM. Thirteen hundred miles away, a Dassault Falcon 200 was already in the sky, screaming south, above the clouds at over four hundred miles an hour. Earlier in the day, Dash and Reggie were unclear about their fate. Now, they were being greeted by Captain Gil Chapman, and his staff of researchers.

An undergraduate at James Cook University, the Aussie finished his Masters in Marine Science at University of Hawaii, Hilo, and was now the top dog at Ocean Watch. With tightly cropped hair and bright eyes, his handshake was firm. "Hi guys. Welcome to Glover. I understand there's a plane on the way. Looks like you won't be getting a chance to hang around."

Dash smiled, grateful to be on firm ground, visibly

uncomfortable in the bright yellow sweat pants, flip-flops, and Glover Research polo given to him after the rescue. "Looks that way. Listen, I can't thank you enough for all that you've done."

Chapman, with his hands on his hips said, "Don't mention it. We all heard the Coast Guard's distress call. Captain Hernandez was anchored up inside the reef hiding from that blow that came through. He's the one who decided to poke his head out and look for you. Captain tells me you lost the rig? You two are lucky. That was one hell of a storm."

"Yes, it was," Dash said. "We're very lucky."

Reggie tried her best to transform into a puff of smoke. Sheepish and quiet, like waking up from a tranquilizer dart, heavy with the realization that her existence would have to be explained and dreading the explanation.

Chapman directed them into the crew lounge, the room dense with the smell of fresh coffee. He spoke in quick bursts with a flashing smile at the end of each puff, "You two make yourselves at home. Your ride should be here in about an hour, give or take." Dash and Reggie nodded thank yous.

When Chapman left the room, Dash monitored Reggie, "You okay?"

"Yeah," she lied.

"Nah...c'mon. Tell me what's goin' on."

"Dash, does anybody know I'm coming? Does

anybody know...I exist?"

Dash hadn't thought this far, "Jules knows you're coming."

Reggie recoiled, "Your ex-wife?"

"Yeah," Dash said, pouring a cup of coffee, drawing a long sniff. "My ex-wife. She happens to be an incredible human being." He slurped. "Want a cup?" Reggie nodded her head yes. Dash hated to wear flip-flops, especially the cheap ones. He kicked them into the corner. "Sit down," he said handing Reggie her coffee.

"I gotta tell ya, Reg...none of this was supposed to go down. I was supposed to get to the island, meet up with you and Chooch, and spread the ashes. Then I was gonna get on a plane back to Nashville and fade off into the oblivion." Reggie was sipping and gently chewing the rim of her styrofoam.

Dash continued, "I guess I'm gonna lay it all out. You deserve that." Reggie looked at him, confused. "Your dad made arrangements. Three hundred grand...in cash. I had Gary set up an offshore account for you. Non-traceable. I've been trying to tell you about it for three days."

Reggie squinted, trying to understand. "What? Three-hundred...I don't want his fucking money. I just wanna go home."

"Listen—don't be an ass. This is a do-over for you. You can make an honest go of it now. It takes the pressure off. I was afraid to tell you. I thought..." he hesitated, "ah, shit...I'm not gonna pull any punches, Reg. I thought if you got the money, you go half-cocked and...piss it away."

Reggie stood up, pacing the room in her rescue ensemble. Then she said, "On what?"

"Drugs. Booze. Whatever the hell it is you've been doin' down there for the last ten years. Can you blame me, Reg? I'm sorry—I worry about cha, I can't help it."

Reggie sat beside a suspect Dash. He recoiled. "If you try to hit me, I'm gonna knock you out."

Reggie leaned in and gently kissed Dash on the cheek, just in front of his ear. The ear still ringing from the shot she gave him the day before. It threw him off.

"What the hell's that for?"

"For giving a shit about me," she said. And then—she stood up and walked out.

The twin Honeywell 6As had barely spun down to idle before the door dropped. 6:03 pm. The snap tight, uniformed co-pilot greeted Dash and Reggie. The refuel at Dangriga took less than thirty minutes. Chapman and his staff gave them an unceremonious send-off alongside Captain Hernandez and the crew of the Sacred Marie. By 6:30pm, they were back in the air.

Reggie was visibly distressed. Dash broke the ice. "This is one hell of a plane, ay, Reg? I guess selling 25 million records'll get you a jet." Her ice wasn't going to break so easily. He continued, "I need a drink. You?"

Making his way to the impressive in-flight bar, Dash was met by the young co-pilot.

"Mr. Nelson," he said, handing Dash a box. "This is from your wife. She met us before takeoff, said to make sure you got it." Then he turned and disappeared through the cockpit door. Dash looked to Reggie, eyebrows raised. "Well, I'll be..." he tore into the well-packed box.

"No shit?!" He said, producing a pair of soft, faded jeans. Digging further, "My favorite shirt! Clean skivvies." Like a kid at Christmas, "My boots—" he said lovingly. "That woman...my god. What the hell was wrong with me for thinking I could live without her."

"I've been meaning to ask you about that," Reggie said, peering over the box to Dash.

"Reg—sometimes we do dumb things. We had too many people living in our relationship. I didn't take the time to kick 'em all out. You start believing things that aren't true. Start to see things that aren't there." Dash pulled out a pair of women's jeans. "That's the short version, anyway."

Jules had packed a pair of her own, guessing at a size. Reggie's face clouded, her lip quivered. "Oh my god."

He wasn't finished. "Here," he said, handing Reggie a flowered sundress, several pairs of new women's underwear, bras, make-up and some sandals. "Something's gotta fit. And...anything's better than these freakin' sweat pants."

He felt something else rattle in the bottom of the box. Beneath all the clothes was a bottle of the 'good-stuff.' Dash guffawed, "Oh! Jules you're an angel from heaven!" Around the bottle was taped a note:

Hi Guys,

I took the liberty to pack some things I thought might make your arrival into the circus a little more comfortable. Reggie, I'm sorry if I got it wrong. I was shooting in the dark without knowing your sizes. Hopefully the jeans fit. If not, maybe the dress. Fingers crossed. I can't wait to meet you and welcome you to our family.

Dash, please be sober when you get here. And look in the forward closet.

Love you
J

forty-four

When Dash reached the forward closet, he paused at the door knob. He contemplated for a moment those old cans of peanuts loaded with a spring. He expected some sort of ghost to tumble forth when he jerked the narrow door. Nothing of the sort was in that closet. Just his favorite, bent, stained cowboy hat. Jules hated that hat. She'd been trying to burn it for years.

Dressed in his signature jeans, boots and denim shirt, he sat next to Reggie. She had decided on the sundress. Her hair was up on her head, as best it would stay. She had done her eyes with mascara, she powdered her face and painted her toenails. She looked on the verge of tears.

"I'm not ready," she said.

"Yes you are. You look beautiful"

Reggie wiped her eyes, "Don't make me cry. This shit

probably ain't waterproof."

Dash chuckled, "If I know Jules—"

Reggie chimed in and they said in unison, "It's waterproof."

The plane made its approach to J.C. Tune Airport at 10:45pm. Clear skies, no wind. As the jet got to within a few hundred yards of the runway, Dash peered over Reggie, out the window. The airport was aglow in the familiar hot lights that accompany film sets, crime scenes and hot news events. He felt for her.

Feet above the runway, Reggie grabbed Dash's hand and let out a long, steady breath. She stared a hole through the forward bulkhead as the wheels hit, closed her eyes and flexed hard against the seat. Dash's hand was white; going numb.

The jet slowed so quickly they skidded forward on the leather seats. Pressed hard into their lap belts. Dash pulled the window shade down, but not before catching a glimpse of the massive crowds that were gathered at the small terminal. As the plane taxied slowly, he unbuckled his seat belt and went to the bar. He poured, over ice, two measures of the scotch from Jules and returned to the seats. Reggie was a mess.

"Here."

"I don't drink that crap," she said.

"C'mon. Nectar of the gods." He said, holding it out for her. "When you get to the gates of Heaven and St.

Peter tells you to go to hell, you'll smell it on his breath."

Reggie laughed a laugh that needed to come. She snorted. Then she sipped the 12-year and made a raunchy face. "Delicious!" She said, coughing, exaggerating.

Dash leaned over and lifted a window shade. The news vans and satellite dishes were glowing along the fence. The engine whine diminished. It went quiet. The pilot emerged from the cockpit, greeted Dash with a handshake, "Mr. Nelson. Ma'am. I apologize for not greeting you in Dangriga, but I was ordered to turn the jet over as quickly as possible."

"We understand. Thank you. 'Preciate you going outta the way."

"No problem, sir. Mr. McGraw said to get it done. I trust you got the package from Mrs. Nelson." Dash gestured to his outfit. "We did. Thanks again."

Patting the back of Reggie's seat, the pilot said, "This is where we leave you two. There are a few officials that need to speak with you. They've requested all unnecessary parties clear out. Myself and first officer Parker are those parties."

Dash nodded, "I expected as much. It's gonna be a long night."

The pilots nodded and descended the stairs. Through the window, three spotless—even in the dark— Suburbans sped towards the plane. No headlights.

Blacked-out, shiny bugs. One of the massive vehicles swallowed the two pilots immediately and sped back to the terminal.

Dash and Reggie waited. She trembled in the seat next to him as she heard the truck doors close, then ascending   footsteps.
Dash rattled his ice. "You ready?"

Reggie, nervous, unsure and afraid, uttered a quick, childlike, "Nope."

forty-five

The nodding donkey that was Reggie's knee pumped faster than the pistons in a Harley V-twin. She couldn't sit any longer. "I can't do this," she said. "I'm gonna be sick." She headed for the aft toilet. Special Agent Watts poked his head into the cabin just as the last wrinkles of her sundress disappeared.

"Everything alright in here?" he said, his quarterback frame hunching to clear the encroaching headliner. Dash stood up to greet him. Another agent filed in behind Watts. Two more agents took up residence at the bottom of the stairs.

"Dash Nelson," he said, extending a hand.

"Hello, Mr. Nelson, Special Agent Watts. Welcome back." Watts gave Dash a firm shake and gestured to the agent behind him. "This is Special Agent Dent." Dent nodded and shook Dash's hand.

Dash sat. Watts scanned the cabin as he unbuttoned his blazer. "Mr. Nelson, I was told there were two souls on board." Dash sipped his scotch.

"Call me Dash. She's in the bathroom—in back," he said, tossing a finger over his shoulder. At that precise moment, Reggie pushed too hard. The bathroom door flew open, slammed hard into the bulkhead, and shut again.

Dash, Agent Watts and Dent were all staring when she emerged. She looked like a frightened cat. While still staring at Reggie, Dash said, "Agent Watts, this is Reg—." He stopped himself, realizing he was going to have to use her real name. He never called her by her birth name. It caught him off guard.

"This is Regina. Regina Collins. She's Paul West's daughter."

Tears welled up in Reggie's eyes. Dash smiled at her. Proud like. "C'mere Reg," he said. Agent Watts and Dent shook Reggie's cold, clammy hand. She sat. A mannequin with painted eyes.

Four leather captain's chairs, two forward and two aft were separated by a heavily varnished mahogany table. Dash and Reggie sat next to each other; Watts and Dent across, facing them. Watts spoke first.

"Ms. Collins, do you happen to have any ID?"

Reggie pulled her crumpled purse from the floor. With it in her lap, she rummaged through its contents to produce, much to Dash's surprise, a bent, tattered passport. Washed a hundred times, crammed into back pockets, and trampled by a heard of wild boar; she handed the mess to Watts. "It expires in two months," she said.

Dash was staring at the side of her face. He now knew why she was unwilling to let that purse from her sight. Watts flipped through it as if he were handling the Magna Carta, to the page with her photo. She was a beautiful young girl.

Reggie said, reaching into her purse, "I was sixteen." She handed Watts another tattered document. With a look of surprise, Watts said, "Your birth certificate? You...always keep a copy of your birth certificate in your purse?"

Reggie said, matter-of-factly, "Yeah. Never know when you're gonna have to jet."

Dash smiled at Reggie. "I'm impressed," he said.

Watts handed the papers to Dent. "Can you confirm Ms. Collins' information? I need a word with Mr. Nelson.

Dash cut in, "Call me Dash. Please."

"Mr. Nelson," Watts stood and stepped into the isle, "I need to ask you some questions. Can we step into the cockpit?" Dash didn't move. "Whatever it is you need to ask, sir, you can ask in front of Reggie. I got nuthin' to hide."

Watts gestured to the open cockpit door, "I'd rather not. Sir? Mr. Nelson."

Dash brushed past Watts and headed into the cramped cockpit. Agent Watts buttoned his blazer and thrust his hands into his front pockets. "Is anyone hungry? Should we have something brought in?" Reggie shook her head. Dash shouted from the cockpit. Watts smiled, "Okay then. We're gonna get this door buttoned up and some AC going."

Watts entered the cockpit to find Dash sitting in the captain's seat, facing forward, messing with some toggles and studying the instrument panel. He tried to lead in with some light conversation, "Nice plane, right?"

Dash nodded, "Mm-hm. Twenty-five million records...buys a lot of cheese." Watts chuckled as he pulled a small digital recorder from his blazer. Dash shifted in his seat.

"Mr. Nelson," Watts pushed the record button and placed the recorder on the instrument panel, "you don't mind if I record this, do you?"

Dash shook his head. "Nope. I don't mind."

"Okay, just for the record, you are one William-Henry Nelson. Correct?"

If looks could kill, Watts would be fertilizer. "Yeah...I'm William...Henry...Nelson. And, I'm officially requesting you call me Dash." Leaning in so his lips just barely touched the small recorder he spoke, "Copy? Loud-n-clear? Check...one, two. It's Dash—just Dash."

Watts grinned a tight-lipped smile. "Okay, Dash." Watts flexed his eyebrows, "How'd you get the name Dash?"

"Really? This is why we couldn't speak in front of Reggie? This is some racy stuff." Dash was good at many things. Controlling the projectiles of his frustration was not one of them. "Well...my father named me William Nelson. William-Henry Nelson. You wanna go through life as the *second* Willie Nelson? I never liked the name Hank, either. When I was a kid, my brother started calling me Dash. He thought it sounded better than Hyphen."

"Ah," Watts said. "I get it. Dash...hyphen. Interesting."

Dash nodded sarcastically. "Yeah. White light interrogation type stuff here."

Watts' smile matched Dash's sarcasm. "Okay, Dash. You win. You want a fast ball?" His smile went slack, "What happen to Paul West's body?"

Dash nodded his head in approval, "Okay...now we're cookin' with gas." He turned sideways in the chair; craned his knee over the armrest and said, "It died."

forty-six

Reggie's flower began to open a bit with Agent Dent. He asked his questions. She answered. He entered those answers into his laptop. He was kind and younger than Watts, with a better approach.

"Okay Ms. Collins. Let me just confirm what I've got here. Date of birth, 08/19/1990. Place of birth, Nashville, Tennessee. Current residence, Bonacca, Honduras, passport number 31195855?"

"Yep. Now what?"

Leaving the screen up, Dent pushed the machine aside. "Well, I sent your info to our database. If you're a bad guy...girl, a bunch of whistles and red lights'll go off. If everything checks out, you'll be good to go. It's just a formality."

Reggie was looking towards the cockpit, "What's up with Dash? Why the secret conference up there?"

Dent deflected the question, "Protocol. I'm not at liberty to discuss the case."

"Case?"

Dent changed the subject, "Can I ask how you go from living in Nashville to living in Honduras?"

She shot back, "Can I ask why you changed the subject?"

Dent smirked, "Nope."

Reggie didn't want to discuss her life. She abbreviated, "It's a long story. I didn't actually live in Nashville. My mom gave birth in Nashville. It's where my dad lived. She wanted me to be a U.S. citizen. We were only here for a couple months."

Dent nodded, "I have to be honest," he said. "I don't even know where Bonacca is. I've never heard of it...no offense." Reggie laughed.

"None taken. Nobody's heard of it. It's owned by Honduras, but it ain't Honduras. It's its own place. It's beautiful. Small. Everybody knows your business. But...I always felt safe—until last week, anyway."

Dent was flirting with Reggie. Her mind was everywhere else. His email pinged.

"Well," he said, perusing the message on his screen. "Looks like you check out. You are indeed, Regina Collins."

"Shit, I was hoping you were gonna tell me I was Jennifer Aniston."

Dent laughed, "Nah, you're much prettier."

"Oh please. You're so full of shit." Dent didn't try again.

forty-seven

The temperature in the cramped cockpit was that of a small meat locker. The glib answer from Dash caused tiny stalactites of dismay to form from the tip of Watts's Roman nose. He shook his head.

"Dash, the morgue attendant left you in the room with Westie's body. He said you requested some 'time with your buddy,'" flexing air-quotes. "When he returned, you were gone. Westie...was gone. Bodies don't just float off into space."

Dash growled, "Agent Watts, you don't get to call him Westie. You didn't know the man. He wasn't a friend. You don't give a shit about West or his body. If nothing else, Special Agent Watts, let's be clear on that."

"Okay, Dash...let's forget Mr. West for the moment. Let's get to the money. The three-hundred-thousand dollars that was transferred out of the country."

"That's none of your goddamn business."

"Really—the Justice Department doesn't feel the same way. Money laundering, secret real estate transactions...terrorist organizations."

Dash couldn't contain his laugh, "Terrorist organizations! Man...I'm a songwriter and I don't give a flying fuck about the Justice Department. Secret real estate? Money laundering?"

Dash got close to Watts, "You've been watching too many movies. Get yourself a hobby." Watts stood up in the cramped cockpit, regretting immediately the attempted intimidation tactic. He looked like a Ken doll that had been tossed from the garage roof. His body bent awkwardly, his limbs dangling.

"I spoke to Charlie Tate. I went to see Terrance Banally."

Dash nearly spun his own head clean off turning it to address Watts. "Hok'ee? You went to see Hoke? At the Ranch? You called him Terrance?" He shook his head, blew out a soft whistle, "How'd that work out?"

Watts diverted his gaze. "He—told me to get the fuck off his property."

Dash guffawed. "Hok'ee said 'fuck?' Wow...he never cusses. I guess flexing your FBI muscle on sovereign land didn't go over too well."

Dash continued. Serious-like. Sans smirk. "Look...Watts. I know you have a job to do, but it's been a real long week. I lost my best friend." Gesturing to

Reggie through the closed cockpit door, "We almost died...a couple times. I wanna see my wife. I wanna pet my dogs. I wanna go home. The money is clean. West is gone."

He picked up the small recorder and brought it close to his lips. "I'm not talking any more about Paul West. You can keep me on this plane 'til the Queen of Shiva pops out my ass. I'm done talking about West." Handing the recorder to Watts, Dash sat back in the captain's chair. "If you're hell-bent on continuing this little dance, let's get official. I want my lawyer."

Clicking off the recorder without a word, Watts took his frame to maximum hunch and opened the cockpit door. Dash followed him into the cabin where they joined Agent Dent and Reggie. Watts was in the fourth quarter, down by a touchdown, and the clock was not his friend.

"Agent Dent," he said glaring across the table to Reggie. "What do we know about Ms. Collins." Dash made an intentional ruckus filling his glass with ice. His slurp was audible. He leaned back into the leather-trimmed bar and crossed his legs. Watts was about to chuck a Hail-Mary.

Dent tried to ignore the tension. "She checks out," he said. "We've heard back from the Honduran consulate, and...aside from a five-year-old misdemeanor, she's clean as a whistle." He smiled at Reggie, hoping for another shot. "She is indeed the daughter of one Rachel

Collins and Paul West."

Watts couldn't hide his sarcasm, "Wonderful!" he said, with a heavy pat on the back for Dent. Reggie jumped when Watts' phone rang. It barely finished the first set of loud tones. Watts' expression revealed everything. He was not eager to take the call.

"Watts," he said curtly. A muffled voice could be heard drifting away as Watts quickly stepped to the back of the plane. Dent, Dash and Reggie watched him rub his brow, bend and glance out the windows. His speech was low, tense. "Yes—I'm...yes, sir. I understand. Crystal clear, sir." Watts didn't need to hit the 'end call' button.

Still staring out the window, he tucked the phone into the pocket of his slacks, and gently sauntered back to join the others. Having still not said a word, he re-buttoned his blazer, pulled at the lapels and brushed the sleeves.

Dent was looking to Watts for instruction. Dash was studying Watts for signs of what just occurred. Reggie shot glances to anyone who would acknowledge with eye contact. Watts pulled the Windsor knot tight against his Adam's apple, turned and released the door.

When the door opened, the raucous crowd roared, "DASH! DASH! DASH! DASH!"

Watts gestured to the agents below. Cold and quietly he said, "Stand by, gentlemen. Game on." Dash's Rolex showed almost midnight.

Reggie darted the short distance to meet Dash at the bar as he gulped the last of his drink. "Game on? What's that mean? You can't leave me here!"

"I'm not goin' anywhere without cha." Dash caught the eye of Agent Dent.

Just then, Watts stepped back from the door and gestured for everyone to get up. "Folks, this party's over." Dent closed his laptop. He was as confused as Dash and Reggie.

"Agent Watts, you care to tell me what's going on, sir?"

Watts was standing with his hands on the back of Dent's chair. "Well Agent Dent, that was the director. Seems our little gathering is playing out in the media more like a hostage stand-off than a welcome home celebration. Bad press. Hurting our image." Dash smirked as the chants grew louder. Watts eyed Dash. "Looks like we're gonna continue this discussion another time." He tapped Dent's shoulder, "We're done here."

forty-eight

When Dash hit the open doorway, the crowd erupted. Cameras flashed in futility at the expanse of dark tarmac. Dash stood waving from the top step. Reggie tucked in behind him. He turned and forced her under his arm, out into plain view of the lights and cameras. She was shaking like a baby bird.

"Reg," he yelled over the crowd noise. "I'm not sure what your plans are...but...I hope you'll stick around for some normalcy. I'd like to get to know ya. I think Jules would, too." Reggie squinted a smile in the night sky.

Watts, Dent, and the two other agents dispersed quickly. Two of the shiny bugs disappeared through the service gate with great haste. No lights 'til they crossed the tracks and hit the entrance ramp to the parkway. The stealthy beast that swallowed the two pilots an hour before sped towards the plane. It stopped parallel to the stairs. Not wanting the reunion plastered all over the world, Jules ordered the driver to block the stairs. Get close. The voyeuristic crowd howled at their inability to tarnish the moment.

The uniformed driver stepped from the driver's seat. Black, tactical cargo pants tucked neatly into black military boots. Black t-shirt, black cap. A black bug, this one with a black .45mm tucked in his black belt.

Dash looked to Reggie. "He's awful serious." Reggie scowled and formed a gun with her forefinger and thumb and touched it to Dash's chin. "You better behave—bitch." The serious man didn't acknowledge Dash or Reggie as they descended the stairs. He opened the back door of the shiny SUV, revealing one very relieved woman.

Jules exited the Suburban with precision. She hugged Dash hard enough to break any remaining unbroken ribs. Letting go with her right arm, she caught Reggie and reeled her in. The only thing the cameras caught was the top of Dash's head as her jubilant greeting immediately knocked that miserable hat off.

She broke the embrace and wheeled back, laughing; teary-eyed. The air seemed to flow into her lungs a little easier. Her tenseness subsided. "Hi honey," she said softly.

Dash couldn't help but laugh. "Jules, this is Reggie—

Westie's daughter." Jules hugged Reggie full on. "Oh my god, Reggie." She said pulling back, "You're so beautiful. The dress! It fit." Reggie was grinning ear to ear. She too felt the air in her chest a little easier. She felt welcomed.

Dash broke ranks as the two women got into the truck. He wanted to greet his fans at the fence. He felt his thick, solid heels click the tarmac. He realized how good it felt to take solid steps again. The armed driver shadowed him closely, directed by Jules. Dash would have preferred he stay behind.

Dash had to shield his eyes from the flashes. The crowd went ten deep. People were standing on the hoods of cars, cheering. Shouting. Somewhere in the din, *Heavy Clutch* was blazing several decibels above it all.

Its structural integrity was pushed to the max as he drug his hand along the cyclone fence, making contact with the many fingers that thrust themselves through the wire. Local news anchors looked awkward, pressed against the fence with the fans, out of place in their suits, ties, and conservative, non-offensive dresses. Helmet-hard hair-dos doing their best against the enthusiasm. He was amused as they tossed silly questions at him in the midst of such an overt outpouring of love.

Laura Night from News Channel 5 shouted, "Dash, how's it feel to be home?!"

Dash laughed at the ridiculousness of the question. "Look at this!" he coughed, "How do you *think* it feels? It feels fuckin' great!" She winced at his answer. Dash chuckled to a fan at the fence. "Whoops! So much for live TV!"

The door closed behind Dash. The silence of the truck felt good. The cold hum of the air-conditioning. Leather seats. All these folks. All that noise. It wasn't making it into the sanctuary of the shiny black bug. Jules patted his knee. "You okay?"

He smiled.

That smile.

The smile he smiled for the Sacred Marie. The smile he smiled in the photo by the bed.

He gently—with the utmost care—draped his arm around her neck and pulled her in close. She looked into an expression she hadn't seen in years. He kissed her softly on the mouth as if for the first time.

"Yep," he said. "I am—absolutely alright."

forty-nine

With the studio lit, Dash sat across from CNN's Anderson Ellis. The soft, white light from the Keno Flo accentuated the creases in his well-worn complexion. The make-up girl finished her last looks. Allie Hart, Jules, and Reggie stood by the monitor.

While Anderson finished his opening, Dash replaced the moisture in his mouth with a healthy dose of the good stuff. He crossed his legs calmly and listened for the cue. "Dash Nelson. Welcome home."

Dash was in his element. "Thanks, Anderson. It's nice to be home."

Anderson began. "This is a bit of déjà vu. Two weeks ago, Jules Nelson, your former wife, sat where you're sitting. The news of your rescue had just been reported. Now, here you sit. Tonight is a bit different. We're live, so...no cursing." Everyone in the room laughed. "What have the last two weeks been like for you?"

Dash shifted. "Well. It's been like a crazy dream, Anderson. In the words of Mark Twain, the reports of my death have been greatly exaggerated."

Anderson laughed, "Some did report a harrowing demise. Others talked of suicide pacts. Now, we have the sudden appearance of Paul West's estranged daughter." Dash listened intently. Jules and Allie exchanged nervous glances at the monitor. Jules wrapped an arm to steady Reggie.

He focused his question, "I want to be sensitive here but, you are directly connected with the disappearance of Paul West's body. The morgue assistant, who's since become somewhat of a colorful figure on social media, says he left you with the body. When he returned, both of you were gone. How do you explain that?"

Dash drew his thumb and forefinger across his lower lip. "Anderson—Westie had a specific request should he come to an untimely death. I made a promise. I wanted to keep that promise. A cold, steel table was not where I was going to leave the man who's been at my side for thirty years. He was my brother."

The room was eerily still. "So you did steal Paul West's body. And there was, after all, a pact."

Dash was unwavering. "Use whatever words you like."

Anderson didn't expect the answer. The tension was palpable. "Where's the body now?" The question shot from Anderson's mouth before he could reel it back in.

Dash smiled, "It's right here," he said, pointing to the center of his chest. Then he pointed off camera to Reggie and Jules. "It's there, and there. Westie is everywhere, man." Pointing directly at Anderson Ellis, Dash said, "He's right in front of me."

Anderson was flustered. "You've done Jimmy Fallon. But you only played the title track from *Heavy Clutch*. You didn't do a sit-down. You did Saturday Night Live. Again, only performance. No skits. Why?"

"Because the show goes on." Dash said. He was in full regalia. Emboldened. Determined. "West and I worked our asses off on this record. The band. The engineers. It's the best music I've made—the most honest. It deserves to be heard." Anderson let him go on. Dash pulled a cigarette from the stool beside him. Jules covered her eyes. Reggie laughed.

"I'm sorry, man," Dash said. "I know it's a nasty habit. I'm tryin' to quit...but, it ain't gonna happen right now." Anderson nodded. He was giving Dash all the rope he wanted. Social media was ablaze. Allie Hart scanned her phone in real-time. Dash went on. "Shine the lights on the music, not the BS. I didn't wanna sit and talk about that stuff anymore."

"You're doing NPR this week. Do you honestly believe Terri Cross isn't going to ask you about this incident? Is it realistic to think, even for a second, that for the rest of your career, this incident will not be front and center on an interviewer's notepad?"

Dash cocked his head at the question. He admired the long stream of smoke he let loose into the light. "No. It's not realistic. But I'm saying this to you, right now. I will not discuss this any further."

Allie put her head in her hands. Jules rubbed her back. Reggie left the studio, against the assistant directors flailing for her to stop. The commotion didn't fluster Dash. He was unfazed.

"I'm not talking about the body, the riots or the boat. I'm not gonna discuss this death pact crap or the silly ass kid at the morgue. There's a record out there that needs to be supported. A career full of music, stories, people. I refuse to be reduced to a headline. I will not let fantasy supplant the real story of West's life. It will not happen as long as I draw breath. If I never do another interview, I'll be fine with that."

Dash snuffed out his cigarette. Anderson was searching his notes. The lack of interaction was disaster for live television. Dash sat forward as if he was getting up to leave. "Anderson," he said. "I'm gonna give you the last shot. We've known each other a long time." Dash was looking directly into Anderson's eyes. "Ask me the question I know you're dying to ask. Go ahead. It's okay. Anything you want. It's gonna be the last question I ever answer, so make it count."

Allie whispered to Jules. "Did you know about this?" Jules shook her head, "No. I swear. I have no idea what he's doing." Allie was helpless. She tried to throw it to a commercial break but the director waved her off. She could do nothing but watch.

Anderson put the cap on his pen, pushed his glasses up onto his forehead and dropped the yellow legal pad containing all his prepared questions to the floor beside him. He accepted the challenge from his long-time friend.

Being the consummate professional, Anderson Ellis did have one nagging question. The question that everyone wanted the answer to, but no one would ever actually ask. Telegraphing his question with a spry smile, Anderson said, "Dash—call me a skeptic but, some people—check that—a *lot* of people think this whole thing reeks of a publicity stunt. What do you say to them?"

The entire room heard the air escape Allie Hart's lungs. Jules stood motionless. She didn't blink. She didn't dare breathe. Dash smiled that famous smile. Jules grabbed Allie's arm and bowed her head, "Oh god...please let this be over," she whispered.

Dash Nelson said, "Well, Anderson...if it was, it was the best goddamn stunt Westie ever pulled."

Free Burning Man Book Soundtrack

As a special gift to my readers, I've handpicked five songs from my three albums for the official Burning Man book soundtrack, some of whose lyrics are featured in the story.

You can download the soundtrack for free here: chrisdicroce.com/burning-man-soundtrack

Featuring the Songs:

Mama's Iron Hand
Last Letter
Watch It Burn
Too Far For Me To Go
I'll Be A Man For You

About the Author

Chris DiCroce is a critically-acclaimed singer/songwriter and Amazon bestselling author who has been writing in one form or another for over 25 years. After producing three independent records on his own label and touring internationally, including a performance at Farm Aid, a USO tour, and as a supporting act for artists such as Robert Plant, he took a break from music and decided to make a change. In 2012, he sold his Nashville home and everything in it to move aboard a 35-foot sailboat with his wife and dog. He began writing books in pursuit of his lifelong dream of publishing a novel. After two successful non-fiction books, Burning Man is his first novel.

He's currently working on his next project from the jungle somewhere in Central America.

To find out more, visit chrisdicroce.com.